Failing g

fortune in forgotten gold.

SHADOWS AND GOLD

Traveling to the most remote region of China certainly wasn't what Ben Vecchio had in mind for his summer vacation, but when Tenzin suggested a quick trip, he could hardly turn down a chance to keep her out of trouble *and* practice the Mandarin he still struggled with in class.

Of course, Tenzin might not have been clear about everything travel entailed.

Driving a truck full of rotting vegetables and twenty million in gold from Kashgar to Shanghai was only the start. If Ben can keep the treasure away from grasping immortals, the reward will be more than worth the effort. But when has travel with a five-thousand-year-old wind vampire ever been simple?

> *"What's on the agenda for tonight?"*
>
> *"I thought we'd go into Shanghai. Eat some fish. See the lights."*
>
> *"Okay."*
>
> *"Then maybe lure a traitor into the open before he steals my gold."*
>
> *Ben paused, thought, then gave her a nod. "Sure, sounds like fun."*
>
> At least he was practicing his Chinese.
>
> Right?

SHADOWS AND GOLD is the first novella in the Elemental Legacy series.

Praise for Elizabeth Hunter

"Elizabeth Hunter's books are delicious and addicting, like the best kind of chocolate. She hooked me from the first page, and her stories just keep getting better and better. Paranormal romance fans won't want to miss this exciting author!"

— *Thea Harrison, NYT bestselling author of the Elder Races series*

"...A truly excellent blend of action, treachery and romance that ends with a startling plot twist. Hunter is an author to watch!"

— *RT Magazine*

"It is rare an author can create characters so enchanting, a world so captivating or a plot so enthralling that it could make it through more than a dozen books. But Elizabeth Hunter can do it - and she does it in spades. I loved this novella."

— *The Lit Buzz*

Shadows & Gold

An Elemental Legacy novella

Elizabeth Hunter

Shadows and Gold

ISBN: 978-1505407853

Cover art: Damonza
Formatted: Elizabeth Hunter

For information, please visit:
ElizabethHunterWrites.com

For the beginning seems to be more than half of the whole...

–Aristotle, *Nicomachean Ethics*

Prologue

"ARGH!"

Tenzin looked up from her book to see Ben tearing at his hair, his elbows planted on either side of what she knew was his Mandarin textbook.

"I'm never going to get this," he said.

"Yes, you will."

"No, I'm not. It's the tones. I can't seem to get the tones right, and they're going to kick me out of my next class if I can't get them right."

She knew that wasn't good. Chinese was his minor field of study. Political science was his major at the university, and Chinese was his minor. At least she thought that was how it worked.

"You need to practice more." She spoke to him in Mandarin. "From now on, I'll only speak to you in Chinese. That will help."

"Please don't," he said in English.

"I don't understand what you're saying," she answered, smiling. "I do not understand English when you are speaking it."

"You are full of shit," he said in Mandarin. Or at least, that's what he was trying to say. Ben was right. He really needed practice.

Just then, an image on the television caught her eye.

"Ben, turn that up."

He glanced up, confused. "What?"

"The television! What is this program? Turn the

volume up."

She stared as the sound grew on the screen in front of her. Images of crumbled brick and construction equipment filled the screen. Men wearing hard hats and pouring concrete.

"Where is that?" Ben asked.

She whispered, "Kashgar."

This was not good.

"Where?"

Familiar mud roofs and bright doorways. Streets filled with colorful dresses. The images on the screen flipped through her memories along with the fragrance of saffron, charred lamb, and dust.

"Where's Kashgar?"

She leaned forward, ignoring Ben and listening to the narrator.

"In the old town, ancient mud brick homes are making way for modern reconstruction, though the government is quick to reassure both citizens and visitors alike that the unique character of this historic city is central to the improvement plans for the special economic zone that is planned."

"Shit."

Ben frowned at her as an image of collapsed walls flashed across the screen. "Why are you so freaked out? It looks like those places were about ready to fall in. Can you imagine how many people might get hurt? Kids might live in those houses."

Tenzin stared at the familiar old streets, tapping her foot. How safe was it? She hadn't moved that cache in several hundred years, but if they started tearing up enough old streets...

Plumbing lines. Foundations. Modern wiring went underground, didn't it?

"Shit," she muttered again.

If only Nima was still alive. She was always better at making these arrangements. She'd need Cheng's help, but he owed her more than one favor. Nobody moved things by horse or wagon anymore. She'd need... What? A truck? A boat? Cheng had many boats. He could probably get her a truck, too. Then there was the new government to deal with. Human governments liked forms and fees. Tariffs and taxes. There would probably be checkpoints, but she could deal with those.

Irritating humans.

"Tenzin, what are you scowling about?"

She glanced at Ben. Back at the screen. A government spokesman was speaking to a reporter.

Speaking *Mandarin.*

She would need a truck, a boat...

And a human.

What was the American phrase? Something about a lightbulb?

Tenzin looked at Ben. Then she looked at his textbook, still laying open on the table in the den. A smile turned up the corner of her mouth.

She asked, "When does your school start?"

Ben was looking at that book again, chewing on his thumbnail. "Next semester starts... Uh, middle of August."

That was months away. Plenty of time. She stood and walked over to him, slapping his book closed.

"Hey! I was trying to—"

"Study, yes. Admirable. But you know what would be better?"

His eyes narrowed. “What?”

“Practicing Chinese with real Chinese people.”

“Aren’t *you* a real Chinese person?”

“Define Chinese. And person.”

He paused. “I see your point. Why are you—”

“I need to make a quick trip to Xinjiang.”

“Where?”

“It’s a province in China. You can come along.”

His eyebrows went up. “Really?”

“Really. Don’t you think that would be better than studying from books?”

He sat back, suspicion written clearly on his face. “I guess I could stand to practice—”

“Excellent! Just see to your visa and I’ll take care of the rest.”

She walked from the room, mentally composing a note for Caspar to send to Cheng’s secretary. She’d need to tread carefully. The last thing she wanted was to end up in the old pirate’s debt.

“Tenzin?” Ben called from down the hall. “What are we doing?”

“Going to China.”

“For?”

“To practice your Chinese, of course!”

Ben muttered something she was pretty sure he had not learned in a textbook.

Chapter One

BEN VECCHIO LANDED in the Ürümqi Diwopu International Airport at ten in the morning not knowing what time it was or what time it was supposed to be. Despite its vast territory, the entire People's Republic of China was on one time zone. Beijing time. You might be in Yunan province, Xi'an, or the Tibetan plateau, but you were still on Beijing time.

He roused himself and, ignoring his snoring seat mate, shoved his way into the aisle to grab his bag from the overhead bin. Personal space, he had quickly learned when he landed in Asia, was not a universal value. He stretched his cramped legs and barely winced when the formidable grandmother in front of him knocked him on the jaw with her suitcase.

She said something to him in what he guessed was Uyghur. She said it again, scowling at his clueless look.

"I'm sorry. I don't understand," he said in Mandarin, the language he'd been practicing for three years.

Three years and he was still struggling. For the perfectionist he'd become under the training of his adopted uncle, Giovanni Vecchio, it was unacceptable. Ben was hoping this trip would finally cement the language in his mind. Flip whatever switch was holding him back from true fluency.

The old woman gave him an odd look. She cocked her head and looked him up and down. Frowned again, then turned her back. Ben cautiously glanced around the plane, only to realize something astonishing.

He blended in. That's why the old woman had given him a strange look. She had expected him to understand her.

Taking a deep breath, the tension in his shoulders relaxed, and Ben felt more at ease than he had in days.

"*Xièxiè*," he murmured to the pretty flight attendant as he shuffled off the plane, hiking his backpack on his shoulder. He strode through the heated tube of the jetway, wondering how hot it would be outside.

It was late summer, and Beijing had been an oven he was happy to leave. He wanted to go back to the city when he had more time—the energy had been intoxicating—but maybe he'd pick spring. Or fall. Maybe even the dead of winter. Anything but the end of June. But Ürümqi was higher elevation and inland. According to what he could find online, Ben was expecting weather a lot like Los Angeles. Warm during the day, but cooler at night. Nothing near the sauna-like conditions of the Chinese coast.

He checked the forecast on his phone as he walked. Mobile phones were as common in China as they were in Southern California, and everyone he'd seen, from the flirting schoolgirl to the Buddhist monk in saffron robes, had one. The vampires, of course, would not.

But so far, he hadn't seen too many of them.

Being a human raised by vampires had its perks. He had sole access to the computer and assorted electronic gadgets in the household. He had little to no supervision during the daytime. And he'd been raised in the kind of luxury since the age of twelve that most of the world could only dream of.

Of course, he'd been under threat of death from his aunt and uncle's enemies for just as long.

By the time he was fourteen, Ben Vecchio knew how to wrestle an opponent twice his size to the ground. By the time he was fifteen, he could shoot an array of firearms, fence with reasonable skill, and use a knife to kill someone in complete and utter silence.

He'd killed a man at sixteen, but it hadn't been silent.

In the five years since it happened, Ben managed to avoid violence whenever possible. And other than an unfortunate run-in with some Russian-Mexican earth vampires, he'd managed pretty well. He liked the rush, but at heart, part of him was still his mother's son. Being noticed made him squirm. He enjoyed surprising people. Flirting around the corners of their awareness until he won. It didn't much matter what he won. Money. Girls. A stupid bet. Ben liked winning, but he didn't like attention.

Which made traveling in Asia something of a shock.

As he walked to collect his bag, he noticed it again. No one looked. No one stared.

"Maybe my favorite place in China so far," he muttered.

It was an uncomfortable thing for him, to be so visible. And in China, he was visible in more than one world. Being the adopted son of two prominent immortals required a visa of a completely different sort than the official government variety. His Aunt Beatrice was the one who'd contacted the Elders at Penglai Island with the information he'd be traveling in their territory "for educational purposes." Since his aunt had been given the title of scribe on Penglai Island, her word was good enough.

Giovanni had still warned him.

"That region is unstable in the immortal world. It always has been. Be careful. Even the Elders keep vampires in Xinjiang on a very long leash. Don't draw any attention to yourself and don't piss anyone off."

He'd only spotted two vampires since he'd arrived. Once at the airport in Beijing and once outside his hotel. Then he'd caught a plane for Ürümqi and hadn't seen one since.

Of course, the sun hadn't gone down yet.

He wasn't quite sure what anyone knew about Tenzin. Tenzin was, as always, vague in her movements. But Ben knew her sire was one of the Elders, so he figured she'd be okay.

For once, it wasn't the vampires making him feel out of place for being human.

His looks—fair skin with an olive undertone, dark curly hair, the thick-lashed brown eyes his mother had given him—marked him from everywhere and nowhere when he was traveling in much of the world. He could be Italian, French, or Middle Eastern. South American or Greek. It was a convenient appearance he'd come to appreciate as he grew older.

He'd been stuck just around six feet for two years, so he figured he'd finished the growth spurt that hit him in high school. Not bad, considering his bastard of a father was a midget. His mother had claimed her brothers were tall, regal men who charmed the beauties of Beirut.

His mother had claimed a lot of things.

But Ben's everyman appearance did nothing for him in China. He was a Westerner. Everyone looked at him. Many gawked. A few even took pictures of him instead of the old palaces the one day he'd spared to visit the Forbidden City.

But in Xinjiang...

The more he looked around as he waited by the luggage claim, the more he realized that many of the men here didn't look Chinese. There were plenty of Eastern Asian looks, but there were Central Asian features, too.

A lot of them.

And... a lot of the Uyghur language.

He'd been sleeping most of the flight, but the more he listened, the more he heard a language he had no idea how to decode.

"Well shit," he muttered. He'd come to practice his Chinese, only to find out half the population didn't seem to be speaking it. As he walked through the arrivals gate, he heard very little Mandarin at all. The people greeting friends and relatives appeared to be predominately Uyghur. A few Chinese. A few foreign business people. But his flight seemed to be mostly a mix of Central Asian looks and languages.

He sighed. "Tenzin."

Go to Xinjiang to practice his Mandarin, huh? Typical.

Ben grabbed his bag and walked toward the exit doors.

He should have known better. After all, Xinjiang was the Uyghur Autonomous Region. For some reason, he figured everyone would still be speaking Mandarin. Because it was China, and everyone spoke Mandarin, right?

His aunt and uncle would say this was why proper prior research was so important.

Lesson learned, Gio.

The intense summer sun hit him the minute he

stepped outside. Ben knew Tenzin was in the city, but he had no idea where she was staying. She'd left him a note the day after she suggested he come to Xinjiang with her. The note was... well, also typical Tenzin.

Ben—

Meet me in Ürümqi in two weeks.

Stay at the Sheraton. The beds won't be horrible.

I'll meet you there.

Tenzin never signed her notes because he knew her handwriting—when she wasn't forging something—and who else would suggest he randomly fly to the most remote city in Asia?

Three old women carrying lighters approached him as he walked down the steps.

"Lighter?" they asked. "Five *kuai*." One asked in Chinese, the others in what he could only assume was Uyghur.

He shook his head. He wasn't even a smoker and he knew that was a rip-off. He might blend in more in Xinjiang, but he still had "foreigner" written all over him to the street merchants.

Street merchants were smarter than most. The former thief in him knew that.

Two of the women wandered off when he shook his head, but one cackled at him and said in Chinese, "One then. Just one *kuai*."

"One, I'll buy." He pulled a small bill from his pocket. Having fire came in handy whether you smoked or not.

"You speak Chinese?" she asked, handing him one of the less worn lighters. "You are young! You are American?" She glanced at his bag. "English? Where are you staying? You need a car?"

"I speak Chinese," he said. "I'll take a taxi, thank you." He took another step toward the taxi line.

"Bah." She frowned and stepped to block him. Not too forceful, but just forceful enough. She was good. "Bad drivers, every one of them. My grandson is here. He'll take you in his car. Only twenty *kuai*."

"You don't know where I'm staying."

"You stay in the city center?"

He didn't want to tell her exactly where, but he scanned the parking lot and saw a young man in a newer car watching them hopefully. He was about Ben's age and didn't look Chinese.

"I'm staying downtown," he said.

She nodded. "Twenty. It's very fair."

"And?"

"And nothing. He is a good driver. You will call him if you need a car again in Ürümqi."

Ben glanced at the boy again. He didn't know how long he'd be staying. Didn't know where he'd be going. A taxi would take him to the hotel and drop him off after he paid the meter, but someone his own age looking to make some extra money might be a good resource. Money he had. Familiarity with the city, he didn't.

He adjusted his backpack and scanned the area for pickpockets. Still no sign. The soldiers with automatic weapons by the door probably discouraged them. There would be easier pickings in the marketplace.

Ben asked, "Does your grandson speak Uyghur?"

"Of course. And Chinese. And a little English. He's very smart. He knows the city very well. You speak English?"

"Yes."

She nodded and herded him toward her grandson. "You practice then. You speak Chinese to him. He speaks English to you. Yes? Good."

Ben smiled and let her herd him. They passed the line of taxi drivers who yelled at the old woman. She ignored them and led him toward the parking lot, where the young man was waiting with a smile and an open car door.

"This is Akil. He is a student at the university. And a very good driver."

Akil held out his hand. "Very nice to meet you," he said in English.

"*Nǐ hǎo ma*?" Ben asked.

"I am well," Akil responded in Chinese as he took Ben's suitcase. "And you? Where can I take you today?"

The old woman had wandered away, no doubt to sell more lighters or find more passengers for another "grandson" who was also the best guide in Ürümqi. He shouldn't be so cynical, but life had taught him that very little was ever as it appeared. Akil seemed to know a couple languages, his car was well-kept, and he didn't have the darting eyes of a con. Probably, he was just a student looking for some extra cash. Ben was more than happy to give it to him, rather than one of the hard-eyed taxi drivers.

They settled in the car and Akil turned up the air-conditioning, though the weather wasn't unpleasant. A little warm, but dry and breezy.

"You can take me to the Sheraton," he said.

"Ah, a very nice hotel." Admiration was in Akil's eyes. "And near the museum. Do you prefer to speak English or Chinese?"

Ben smiled. "What's your best language?"

"Uyghur," he said with a laugh. "But then Mandarin. School, of course."

"Are you in university?"

"Yes, in Qinghai. I am studying agriculture."

"Really?"

"Yes," Akil continued in flawless Mandarin. "It is very important. My family has orchards, but we want to be more modern. To make our farm more successful."

"Cool," Ben muttered.

"Cool," Akil copied him in English, grinning.

Ben smiled back. "How old are you?"

"Twenty-two. And you?"

"Twenty-one."

"What is your name?"

"Ben."

"Welcome to Ürümqi, Ben."

"Thanks."

"Why do you come to Xinjiang?" Akil asked in English.

"I'm meeting a friend here."

"Is he Uyghur?"

"She's... sort of Chinese. But she lives in Los Angeles now."

"Los Angeles!" Akil exclaimed. "Hollywood. This is where you live?"

"Yes, but I'm not in Hollywood. I'm just a student, like you."

"What do you study?"

"Political science and Mandarin. I thought it would be good to come to China to practice speaking Mandarin."

Akil started to laugh. "You came to Xinjiang to practice Chinese? Why didn't you go to Beijing? Or Xi'an?"

"I'm starting to think my friend had ulterior motives."

"I think you are right."

Fifteen minutes later, Akil dropped him off at the front of the hotel, ignoring the dismissive look of the doorman in attendance. Ben caught it, but the man was nothing but politeness for Ben, whom he greeted in English.

"Checking in?"

"Yes, thank you." The doorman whisked his bag away as Ben turned to pay Akil.

"Here." The young man handed him a card. "If you need a driver—"

"I'll call you," Ben said. "For sure. Any suggestions until I meet my friend tonight?"

"The museum is good," Akil nodded down the street. He'd pointed it out on the way to the hotel. "You can walk there. There are signs in English, which isn't common in Chinese museums. It will give you a good idea of the area's history. And there are the mummies."

"Mummies?"

Akil smiled. "Yes. They're famous. The Loulan girl. You should see them. And if you need a driver or an interpreter—"

"I got it." Ben held up the card. "I'll call you."

Akil held out a hand. "Stay cool," he said in English.

"You too."

He walked into the dry air conditioning of the hotel lobby and glanced around.

Clearly new, the Sheraton in Ürümqi was probably built to appeal to business travelers. Akil had told him that Xinjiang was one of China's fastest growing provinces, even though it was the most remote. The farthest west province of the People's Republic bordered Mongolia, Russia, and Kazakhstan, and more than one guidebook said it had more in common with that Central Asian country than it did with the rest of Han-dominated China.

Ben knew it was a diverse region, dotted by some of the most ancient cities on the Asian trade routes.

He just had no idea why Tenzin wanted him there.

Chapter Two

"HELLO," BEN SAID to the girl at the front desk. Despite her suit, she looked younger than he did, but her manner was completely professional. He gave her his most charming smile, hoping for a reaction. After all, it was summer break. He was on vacation. A guy could use a little fun.

"Can I help you, Mr. Vecchio?"

The desk clerk answered him in English, but he continued in Chinese.

"How are you today?" Something. Anything?

"Very well, sir. How can I help you?"

And nothing. She was the picture of efficient professionalism. Oh well.

Ben had settled into the hotel and debated whether or not to go out in the city or sleep. Being raised by the nocturnal had given him the ability to sleep when he needed to, but he was still affected by jet lag. He had decided to stay up, hopefully stave off the worst of the exhaustion, then sleep in the afternoon. He didn't know when Tenzin would show up, or if the vampire would be forthcoming about her real motivations. But he knew she wouldn't show up until the sun was down. He had to be on his toes so he decided to sleep later.

"I have a few hours before I need to meet a friend," he told the clerk. "What would you recommend that is nearby?"

She pulled out a small map in English. "The Regional

Museum is very good. There is an excellent exhibition on the Silk Road, which is of course very important the history of Xinjiang. There is also shopping next door." She held a polite hand toward the attached luxury mall, which held zero interest to him. He could get all the same things on Rodeo Drive.

"You're the second person to recommend the museum." Another smile that affected her not at all. "I think I'll go there."

"If you take your passport with you, they will likely waive the entrance fee. Since you are a visitor."

"Thank you."

"Of course."

Waive the entrance fee? That was a new one. So far, he'd had to pay to get... well, just about anywhere. Even the *hutong*, the historic neighborhoods in Beijing, asked visitors who were walking through to pay an entrance fee. Was it legal? Who knew? But everyone did it, so Ben didn't argue.

Walking through the luxury mall with its glowing six foot ads and discreet security, Ben started to feel conspicuous again. He saw a few tourists surreptitiously snap pictures on their phones, which made him grit his teeth. It was habit to avoid the camera by now. Giovanni and Beatrice kept a few pictures in the house, but when you were immortal, it was best to not keep around photographic evidence of how much you didn't age. The human brain could convince itself of almost anything—like when the neighbor who had lived quietly in the house down the street didn't look a year older than he had ten years ago—but photographic evidence was harder to dismiss.

He reached the end of the mall and left through the soaring glass doors. New construction surrounded him. He slipped on his sunglasses and scanned the street to find the best place to cross, following the old women who were selling baskets of plums.

According to Akil, Ürümqi was divided between the Han neighborhoods and the Uyghur ones. The museum was in a mostly Han area, but he still saw an intriguing mix of faces. Xinjiang was becoming more and more interesting the longer he visited.

He passed through security at the museum, then walked up the steps and into the cool interior. A glowing map of Xinjiang spread in front of him, and curious groups of Chinese tourists gathered around it, taking turns pressing the lights that highlighted the various routes of the Silk Road. He turned left to follow the crowd.

Ben took his time in the exhibits. He had at least three hours to kill, and the museum looked like it would eat up more than enough. As he toured the hall highlighting the various ethnic groups that made up the province, he scanned the crowd. No one was following him. Other than a few curious glances, no one seemed to pay him any mind.

Nothing suspicious.

He heard a small group mention the mummies that Akil had spoken of, so he followed them.

Up the stairs and around the atrium, Ben headed toward another hall.

The minute he stepped inside, he could feel her.

Tenzin.

She was there. He didn't know how. Or why. But some sixth sense alerted him. It had always been that way with her.

"The Tarim mummies of Xinjiang—" A tour guide caught his attention as she stood before a glass case. "—are only some of the evidence that this province has been continually occupied for over four thousand years. DNA evidence suggests that the mixed populations of the Tarim Basin had origins in Asia, Europe, Mesopotamia, India, and many other regions. This evidence confirms ancient Chinese historians who reported tribes who appeared to be European passing through and even inhabiting these areas. There were reports of tall men and women, with blue and green eyes. Red and blond hair. Even full beards." The group laughed quietly. "As you can see, the population of Xinjiang continues to represent this diversity."

A shadow passed to his right, and Ben walked into another room.

Tenzin was a day-walker. While most vampires needed to sleep for most of the day, a few did not. Beatrice said it was because Tenzin was so old, but Ben knew other old vampires who needed to sleep. Tenzin wasn't like them. She was just as active during the day as humans were. She just couldn't go out in the sun. As long as she kept out of the light, she was fine.

Was it age or something else? He didn't really know. Beatrice had taken a lot of Tenzin's blood because her father and Tenzin had been mated, so Beatrice didn't sleep much either. It wasn't something his aunt liked and she often spent much of the day meditating in the dark while her mate slept.

Ben had never heard Tenzin complain about it.

He couldn't imagine never sleeping. He loved to sleep. Loved to dream. Missing that would make him a little crazy.

He walked quietly through the hall, trailing behind another tour group, stopping when they did, hanging on to the edge of the crowd, listening and trying to ignore the invisible eyes he could feel watching him. He wouldn't see Tenzin until she wanted to be seen.

Ben wandered to the next room, heading over to the first case he saw with a mummy inside. He leaned over, trying to see her features beyond the glare of the protective glass.

*Qiemo Female Mummy,'*the case read. *The mummy was exhumed from No. 2 tomb. Date: 800 BC. Height 160 cm. She belongs to a mixture of Europoid and Mongoloid traits.*

The mummy in the case was remarkably well-preserved, with a deep crimson robe that was intricately sewn. She had swirling tattoos along her face and four thick braids hung past her shoulders. 160 centimeters meant... He did a quick calculation and determined the mummy was over five feet. Taller than he would have expected.

800 BC.

Ben stared at the mummy, thinking of the vampire he could feel in the air around him, as if her ghost hovered over his shoulder.

What had this woman seen? What had her life been like? How old was she when she died? Had she had a happy life? Someone had taken care when they buried her. Her body was carefully positioned and her jaw wrapped with the same crimson thread her robe was made from. Maybe she was a beloved wife. A mother.

The woman in the glass case was almost three thousand years old. Had Tenzin been alive then? Probably.

He didn't really know how old she was. No one talked about it. Then again, no one really knew, did they? Maybe not even Tenzin herself.

He caught a flash of reflection in the glass. A darting glance. A fanged smile. By the time he'd turned around, she was gone.

BEN made his way back to the hotel when the sun began tilting toward the horizon. There was a rush of cold air at the doorway to the mall, then the long lit walk past the store fronts. Cartier. Louis Vuitton. Hugo Boss. The juxtaposition of luxury and history was jarring to the senses. He ducked his head when he saw another phone camera pointed in his direction and kept it down until he'd entered the hotel and made his way to the elevators.

Quiet.

Ben took a deep breath and closed his eyes. The elevator sped to the fifteenth floor without stopping, the dinging doors more welcome than any familiar voice. A few more steps and he was in the generic surroundings of a Western chain hotel thousands of miles from home. Door locked. Chain set. Portable electronic alarm attached to the door.

Quiet.

Ben was used to quiet. He often came home to a house where no one was home or no one was awake. It was soothing.

He plugged his phone into his laptop and quickly downloaded the photos he'd taken at the museum, then erased them from the phone. On the off chance it was hacked, no thief would be able to track his movements by his photo history. Then he logged into the virtual private network he used when he was traveling, checked his email and the secure remote dropbox that Gio and Beatrice had set up, before he reset his passwords for the week and turned the computer off.

The security measures were automatic, a routine that had been drilled into Ben as soon as he learned how to work a keyboard. His aunt had more than a passing ability with computers, and she'd taught Ben if it *could* be hacked, it probably *would* be. But that was more of a human threat.

Vampires, on the whole, distrusted technology. Often, the most important messages or communications still made their way by personal courier. Couriers were as well trained as assassins and just as expensive. Immortals on the whole were paranoid about security, and often sired children or kept humans whose sole purpose was transporting information discreetly. Beatrice's grandfather had a human constantly at his side, loyal to a fault and ready to transport any letter the old vampire might write. Ben knew at least one of Giovanni's regular correspondents who still used wax-sealed scrolls.

There was something to be said for old-school.

He checked his watch and decided to fit in another hour or two of sleep. Ben pulled off his shirt and, glancing toward the sunny window, cracked it open before he went to lay down. Within minutes, he was dreaming.

HE woke when the bed shifted slightly.

Ben kept his eyes closed and took a deep breath.

Dust. Honey. Cardamom.

"Hey, Tenzin."

She scooted further over on the bed and he shifted to make room.

"No, really," he muttered, keeping his eyes shut. "Make yourself at home."

"I told you these beds would be comfortable."

"I wouldn't call this comfortable."

"Comfortable for China, then. You're so American."

"You're so intrusive."

"You left the window open."

"I'm on the fifteenth floor."

She just laughed.

"You realize you have boundary issues, right Tiny?"

"Boundary issues?" She bumped her shoulder into the space between his bare shoulders. "Are you being modest again?"

"Maybe."

"Funny boy. It's not like you haven't seen me naked."

He *had* seen her naked. It had been a defining moment of his adolescence before Giovanni walked out to the pool and lectured Tenzin on modern standards of decency around seventeen-year-old boys. He'd held a grudge against his uncle for weeks.

Ben rubbed his eyes and rolled over. "Hi."

"Hello. How did you like the museum?"

She was wearing her hair in braids which were oddly reminiscent of the mummy he'd seen earlier. He decided not to tell her that. He liked her hair in braids. Tenzin's hair was past her shoulders and thicker than any woman's hair he'd ever seen. Like a black cloud flying behind her when she wore it loose. She often wore it in braids, a habit Giovanni said she'd picked up in Tibet. Sometimes, she tied the ends with brightly colored string that flashed and fluttered when she was in the air. He reached out and tugged on the end of one.

"I liked the museum. It was interesting. How did you get in there?"

"A guard let me in last night. There are some very comfortable yurts in one of the exhibits."

"He let you in? You mean you used *amnis* on the night guard so he would let you in."

"Same same."

"Not really."

Tenzin sat up and folded her legs on the bed as he scooted up to sit against the headboard. He reached for his t-shirt and tugged it on. Ben pulled up his legs and crossed his arms on his knees, settling his chin there as he yawned.

"How old are you?" he asked.

"Old enough to know better and still not care."

He smiled. "No, really."

She cocked her head. "The mummies?"

"Mm-hmm."

"Older. Older than the mummies there."

He mouthed, *Wow*.

"Ancient." She drifted into the air and did a slow roll. "I am an old, old woman."

He loved the way she flew. It wasn't like a bird. Tenzin moved through air as a fish did in water. Second nature. She looked out of place on the ground.

"All right, Bird Girl." He tugged on the end of the loose pants she wore. "Tell me what we're doing here?"

Her eyes flashed to his and she gave him a fanged grin. "What? You wanted to practice your Mandarin, didn't you?"

"Yes, so obviously we went to a place where half the population doesn't even speak it."

"So you can learn some Uyghur, too."

"Tenzin."

She flew up and hovered over him on the bed. "Don't be cross."

"I'm not. I just want to know what we're really doing here."

"I have an errand to run. And I thought you could keep me company."

"What kind of errand?"

She clammed up. Typical.

Ben sighed and leaned back against the headboard. "You know, I heard Xi'an is really nice. And the terra cotta army—"

"All the tourists go to see that. Don't be boring."

"They see it because it kicks ass, Tenzin."

She sneered. "It's packaged history."

"So is any museum. What are we doing here?"

"I just have a few things to take care of, then we can—"

"Tenzin."

"I'll let you know when you need to know."

"Listen," he growled as he leaned forward. "You needed *me* here, otherwise you wouldn't have suggested I come. So tell me now or I'm out of here."

She said nothing, hovering with her back against the far wall, a petulant expression on her face.

He shook his head, swung his legs over the side of the bed and walked to his suitcase. "Packing now. I'll see you back in LA."

"Benjamin—"

"Nope. Done now."

"Don't be like this."

"Like what?" He unplugged his laptop and slid it into the case. "Impatient with your pathological secrecy?"

"You're being immature."

"Nice try, playing that card." He pushed down the loose pants he'd been wearing to sleep and pulled on jeans. "But it stopped working a few years ago. This is not me being immature. This is me being sick of your shit."

"Ben—"

"Xinjiang isn't top on my dream destinations list, so if you don't want to tell me—"

"I need to move approximately twenty million dollars worth of gold and antiquities out of a cache in Kashgar before the old city is demolished."

Ben froze.

"And obviously, I need a human to help me. Since you had time before school started, I thought it would be fun."

She thought it would be *fun*? Of course she did.

He took a measured breath. "Twenty million?"

"Approximately."

"In gold?"

"And antiquities. Some porcelain. Jewelry." She floated down to the edge of the bed. "A few rugs, but those might be damaged."

"Yeah, that can happen with rugs."

She shrugged. "They're silk, so they might still be good. I'm mostly concerned with the gold."

"Twenty *million*?"

"Mostly in gold."

He nodded silently, then went to sit down next to her, rubbing a hand over his face. "When was the last time you moved this cache?"

Tenzin scrunched up her face. "Maybe... two or three hundred years ago? I was still killing vampires with Gio. Sometime then. We had a job in Samarkand, and I had some extra time."

"Of course you did." He cleared his throat. "Two or three hundred years? Are you sure it's still there?"

"There is a family who guards it. They don't know what it is, of course. They just guard it. Nima handled all of that. Of course, I don't know if anyone is paying the family anymore, so they might be gone..." Her eyes were distant for a moment until they snapped back to his. "I forgot about it until that news broadcast."

"You forgot about twenty million in gold?"

She shrugged.

"How many gold caches do you have?"

"You don't need to know that."

Ben took another deep breath and blew it out slowly. "And do you have a plan to get this gold out of the People's Republic of China, who might have a problem with you taking valuable cultural treasures—that are probably worth a lot of money—out of the country?"

She frowned. "But they're *my* treasures."

"I know that, but—"

"*Mine*. I'm the one who..." She considered her words. "...*acquired* them. I stored them. They're mine."

"I realize that, but the government might think differently."

"I have a plan."

Ben nodded. "That's good." *Twenty million dollars?* "Plans are good."

Especially when you're trying to move twenty million

in gold.

Tenzin smiled. “I know a relatively trustworthy pirate who owes me a few favors.”

“A *pirate*? Like, an actual... pirate?”

“Yes!” She seemed delighted. Of course she did. Because pirates were so delightful. “Well, I don’t think he’s a pirate anymore. Precisely. He’s relatively—”

“Trustworthy. Yeah, I heard that part.” Ben stood up and raked a hand through his hair. “Is the sun down? I need food.”

“Oooh!” Tenzin clapped her hands. “Let’s go get noodles. Xinjiang noodles are the best.”

Ben grabbed his wallet and Tenzin’s hand. “Good to know. We’re walking out the lobby. Put your fangs away.”

“Relax. Sometimes, Benjamin, you have no sense of adventure.”

Chapter Three

THEY WALKED THROUGH the market after the sun set, enjoying the smell of spices and cooking oil that filled the air. The night market in Ürümqi was a melange of faces, scents, and colors. Children ran about in brightly colored dresses and shirts. Stylish Uyghur women in intricately embroidered *hijab* surveyed wares with a critical eye. Caps and scarves. Bread and fruit. Everything was for sale in the market that night.

"You fit here," he said, looking around.

"I fit where? China?" Tenzin asked. "I can't imagine why."

"*Here* here. In Xinjiang."

It was true. He'd never been able to place Tenzin's appearance. She was Asian, for certain, but didn't have the typical features of the Han Chinese who dominated the Western view of China. Tibetan? Mongolian was probably closer. He didn't suppose those kind of labels existed in her human years.

Her complexion was pale, but much of that had to do with her vampiric nature. Her eyes were a cloudy grey, but that could have happened during her transformation however many thousand years before. There was no way of knowing what she'd looked like as a human, but she'd been turned in her late teens or early twenties. Of that, he was fairly sure.

And in Central Asia—with its fascinating mix of people—she did, somehow, fit.

Tenzin shook her head, lifting the corner of her mouth in a smile. A hint of her ever-present fangs peeked out. "I don't fit anywhere, Ben."

"Whatever, oh ancient and mysterious one." He nudged her shoulder to head down an alley that smelled particularly savory. "You fit with me."

She raised an eyebrow, and Ben quickly added, "And all the other nocturnal weirdos. You know what I mean."

"I know what you mean. This noodle shop is good." She pointed toward one where a man in a cap was standing outside, cooking skewers of what smelled like lamb over a narrow, rectangular grill. "They have good noodles."

"Is that rice?" There was a large metal cooking bowl, even bigger than a wok, sitting outside over a concrete oven.

"*Polo*," she said. "Kind of like a pilaf. Very common here. Rice, chicken, carrots. It's good. We can have some of both."

She spoke to the man in quiet Uyghur and he held out a hand, guiding them inside where a smiling woman motioned them to a table and seated them with menus that Tenzin ignored. She spoke a bit more with the woman who nodded and disappeared to the kitchen.

Tenzin said, "I ordered a few things. You can try some of everything that way. It's a good thing you like spicy food."

"But did you order *enough*?"

She shrugged. "For your appetite? They might have to kill another sheep."

It was quiet in the restaurant, with only a few tables occupied, mostly by small groups of men. One table was full of children some older women hovered over. They were watching a soccer game on a small television and eating noodles as they laughed and joked. Cousins maybe? Ben knew some of the minority groups in China could have more than one child. Whoever they were, they looked like family and added a cheerful atmosphere to the tiny restaurant.

The walls were decorated with nice artwork in bad frames, but the ceiling was embellished with painted wooden beams that Ben suspected were hand-carved. He and Tenzin drew a few looks, but most of the patrons seemed far more interested in their own conversations.

"This is nice," Ben said, sitting a moment before a pot of tea appeared at the table. It smelled like honey and saffron.

"The food will be good."

"How do you know?"

She smiled. "Because it smells good, silly."

Within minutes, the table was full of dishes. The golden rice dish he'd seen cooking outside, scented by cumin and dotted with raisins and carrots. Noodles topped with lamb and peppers. Small sticks of meat charred from the fire.

"How much of this are you going to want?" Ben asked, his mouth watering.

She smiled. "Not much. Go ahead."

Vampires never had large appetites, but they did eat. Beatrice said that even though blood was all they truly needed, immortals who didn't eat lived with a gnawing feeling in their bellies which was as uncomfortable for them as it was for humans. Since their digestion was slower, they never ate much. Small tastes of things here or there were all they needed.

Tenzin ate regularly, but that was partly because she liked to cook. Ben considered it fortunate that he liked to eat, because he was always available to dispose of the leftovers.

"Oh my gosh," he mumbled around the first bite of noodles.

"I told you."

"I'll never doubt you again."

She smiled. "Really?"

"No, of course I'll doubt you." He set down his chopsticks and picked up the spoon to try the rice. "You can barely operate in the modern world, Tenzin."

She rolled her eyes and took a small bite of a lamb skewer. Ben ignored the eye-roll because they both knew he was right. He may have been young, but he'd assisted Giovanni's butler, Caspar, for years. There were things that had to happen during daylight, and part of his job in the household was taking care of those things. Dealing with contractors and delivery personnel. Going to the market and sometimes paying bills. He'd been helping to run a household since he was twelve.

Tenzin, on the other hand, often had the lights shut off in her warehouse because she forgot to pay the bill. Sometimes, it was days before she noticed. Bookkeeping was not her forte.

"Will anyone understand us here if we speak in English?" he asked.

"Probably not, but switch to Spanish if you want to be careful."

He switched to Spanish.

"So, we're moving a cache of valuables."

"Yes. From Kashgar."

"Which is close to Ürümqi?"

"It's about fifteen hundred kilometers."

Ben almost spit out his tea. "What?"

"It'll take a day of driving or so to get there. The roads..." She waved a hand. "You know."

"No, I don't know." He pushed back the annoyance. This was Tenzin, after all. The whole concept of driving amused and baffled her. "Why did we meet in Ürümqi instead of Kashgar? I saw connecting flights at the airport."

"Because we have to pick up the truck here, of course."

He took a deep breath and closed his eyes, switching back to English and speaking quietly. "Okay, we're starting from the beginning."

Tenzin frowned. "I thought we were at the beginning."

"Tenzin!"

"Okay. So impatient."

She refilled both cups with tea and spooned a small portion of rice onto her plate.

"The person who is helping me has many shipping operations, including some that use trucks. He owes me a number of favors, so he has arranged a truck for us here in Ürümqi."

"Has he arranged permits, too?" He took some more noodles. "I can't imagine that you ship anything in China without a ton of permits."

She waved a hand. "He assures me that the papers are taken care of and will be with the truck, along with a manifesto."

"I think you mean manifest."

"Yes, that. There will be crates with the truck with

vegetables in them. Some of them will be empty. We will use these to pack my things." She ate some of the rice and watched Ben finish off the noodles. He thought about ordering more, but then a second round of meat sticks came to the table.

Score.

Tenzin continued, but switched back to Spanish. "So Cheng has arranged all this here in Ürümqi. He does not have trucks in Kashgar, so we will have to drive it there."

"So, it's a day of driving through what are probably mountains and deserts where I've never driven before."

"Maybe two days," she mused. "I forget you have to sleep."

He rubbed a hand over his face. He needed something stronger than tea.

"Yeah, Tenzin, I have to sleep. So when you say a day of driving, do you actually mean twenty-four hours?"

She frowned. "I think that's what it will be. I'll fly, of course, so—"

"Oh no. You're not flying."

She looked up from her plate. "Of course I am."

"I don't think so. If I'm driving a truck to get *your* stuff, then you're riding with me."

"I do not ride in human vehicles," she said with a sneer.

"Then you can sit on the top of the damn cab, for all I care. But you're not flying your vampire butt to Kashgar in a couple hours while I drive a big-ass truck for two days on my own. If you think that's the deal, then I can catch a flight home tomorrow."

She scrunched up her face. "You are not nearly as cooperative as Nima."

"*Nima* had a staff of people at her beck and call, Tenzin." He was really trying to be patient, but sometimes, Tenzin just pissed him off. "Nima probably had contacts of her own, like Caspar does, who could arrange anything and everything for the right price. You have me. Who you dragged out here on false pretenses—"

"What is false?" she protested. "Your conversational Mandarin is appalling."

"Wh—*appalling*?" His mouth gaped. "It is not appalling!"

She said nothing, just sat back in her chair and pursed her lips in silent judgement.

"Fine," he said. "It's not great. I still think appalling is a little strong. But we're not in Beijing or Xi'an, Tenzin. You brought me here so you could have a human to help you get your stuff."

"So?"

He sat back. "So what's in it for me?"

Tenzin mirrored his posture, crossing her arms over her chest and narrowing her eyes. A slight smile came to her lips. Tenzin *loved* to bargain.

"I'll pay you," she said.

"Not interested. I have plenty of money." It was true. The trust fund Giovanni and Beatrice had set up grew every year, and he'd been investing his own money since he was seventeen.

Her eyes lit up. "You don't want money?"

"Nope."

And he had her. A bargain for something other than money was irresistible.

"What do you want then?" she mused. "What does my Benjamin want?"

He said nothing and let her speculate. Ben also ignored her use of the possessive pronoun, because that wasn't somewhere he needed to go just then.

She leaned forward and sipped the honey-scented tea. "Gold."

"The first thing you're going to agree to is driving with me. If I'm in that truck, then you are, too."

Tenzin cocked her head. "This is part of the price?"

He nodded.

"Very well." She kept watching him. "You don't want gold."

Ben shrugged.

"You want..." Then her eyes smiled. "You want something shiny, don't you, Benjamin?"

She did know him, after all.

Ben had lived much of his life with nothing to carry but the clothes on his back and whatever he could fit in his pockets. A psychologist would probably have a field day with his acquisitive nature, but he knew—even before he met Giovanni—he liked nice things. More than once, he'd escaped his parents and spent all or most of the day wandering through the Metropolitan Museum of Art. It was one of the few places in the city he could get into for free. Plus, it was full of beautiful things.

Then, he'd met Giovanni Vecchio. And Benjamin would be the first to admit that part of the allure the vampire had was the elegant brownstone he owned in Manhattan. Filled with art, antiques, and books, it was a thief's dream.

And when Giovanni told his new charge he could teach him how to get all those pretty things without the police dodging his steps, Ben listened. And he learned. He already had the skills his mother taught him, plus a hefty sense of self-preservation gleaned from dodging his father. Learning for Ben came easily. But while his Uncle Giovanni's truest love in the world—other than his mate—was books, Benjamin Vecchio's was art.

Paintings. Sculptures. Jewelry of all kinds. The older, the better. And if it had a story attached? Even more irresistible.

So yes, Ben wanted something shiny.

"How much art is there?" he asked.

"Not a lot," she admitted. "But there is jewelry."

"I want my pick. One piece."

"*My* pick. Don't you trust me?"

He grinned. "Not with the good stuff. You're as big a magpie as me. You're talking about two days of driving up to Kashgar. Packing your gold. Then driving all the way to… Where are we shipping this stuff to L.A.?

"Shanghai. Cheng's boats are in Shanghai."

Ben took a deep breath. He was going to be spending a lot of time on the road. He only hoped the paperwork was as good as Tenzin was assuming. His insistence on her riding with the truck was also a practical consideration. If they ran into any trouble, Tenzin—with her flawless Mandarin and ability to influence human thought with *amnis*—would be far more able to handle the police. It would be up to him to make sure things didn't get unnecessarily violent.

In fact, that had been his stated assignment more times than he could count. He could even hear Giovanni's voice in the back of his mind.

"You'll be helping Tenzin on this, Benjamin. Please try to avoid unnecessary violence."

It might even be considered a motto at this point in his life.

Still, Ben shook his head. He knew he had to be firm. Tenzin would take any and ever advantage otherwise. "Tiny, if I'm doing all this driving and packing and more driving, it's my pick. It won't be unreasonable. Don't you trust *me*?"

Tenzin sat back and sipped her tea again. She thought. Sipped some more. Ben was finished talking. He had his pick of a centuries-old treasure cache on the ancient Silk Road on the line. He picked up a skewer of lamb and savored the taste, licking the corner of his mouth when the juices dripped.

"You're right," he said. "Uyghur food is amazing."

"One thing," she conceded. "One piece. And don't piss me off."

He held in the triumphant smile. "Wouldn't dream of it."

"Yes, you would."

"Maybe I'd dream about pissing you off, but I wouldn't actually do it. Not intentionally anyway."

"One piece, Benjamin."

He held out his hand. "You're in the truck with me while we're transporting the goods, and I get one piece of *my* choosing from the cache."

"Agreed."

They shook and then he eyed her plate. "Are you going to finish that?"

"You're a bottomless pit, you know that, don't you?"

"Someone has to finish all this food."

He finished the rest of the food with relish and tried not to show his triumph at the bargain. Tenzin had centuries of treasure in that cache and probably no idea how valuable it was all worth. She didn't read auction catalogues or museum publications.

Neither did most of Ben's friends, but then again, he'd always had unusual interests. He was fine with it.

His best guess was, if Tenzin was valuing the cache at twenty million, it was probably closer to twenty-five or thirty, depending on the condition of the silk. It didn't matter, really. Ben had no interest in selling anything. Whatever piece he chose would be for his own collection.

"You know," she said as she watched him finish the food. "You're the one who fits in here."

He looked up. "Me?"

"You have Persian eyes, Benjamin."

He shook his head. "My mom was Lebanese, not Persian."

Tenzin shrugged. "What does blood know about borders? Persian eyes. You should be happy. They're very beautiful."

"Thanks."

"You're welcome."

Tenzin looked around the restaurant, but no one was staring at them anymore. She leaned back and watched Ben finish his tea. He got out his wallet to pay the bill, wondering if Tenzin was even carrying any modern currency.

Probably not.

Then again, the vampire was going to hand over a priceless piece of jewelry or artwork of Ben's choosing in exchange for his help driving a truck and packing. It may have been more time then he'd planned on spending in China, but how dangerous could it be? All in all, he was happy with the deal.

Dinner could be his treat.

Chapter Four

IT WAS CLOSE to two in the morning—middle of the night for humans, but the heart of the working day for vampires—when they met Cheng's man in Ürümqi. Ben hung back, watching Tenzin from a distance as she talked with the vampire whose eyes kept flicking from Tenzin's slightly hovering form to Ben as he leaned in a small doorway. Ben wore the dark shirt and jeans he'd worn to dinner and carried nothing on him that the vampire would easily detect.

The small knives in his waist had been acquired in the market from a shop above a metalworker who sold copper tea pots on the ground floor. He'd quickly ushered Tenzin upstairs to show her the far more illegal offerings he sold to discreet customers. The revolver on Ben's ankle wasn't fancy, but it was serviceable. As for the more obvious firepower they'd bought, that had been stored back at the hotel. After they left the warehouse where they were meeting Cheng's man, they would stop by the hotel, check out, and get on the road as soon as possible.

According to his phone, driving to Kashgar would take over twenty-three hours, so he was expecting to be on the road for at least two days. Tenzin assured him that the highway was clear, if winding, and they would have no problems traversing it.

Ben knew Tenzin didn't know jack shit about roads, so he wasn't taking anything for granted. Still, she'd also told him that much of the fresh produce in China was grown in the Kashgar region, which made the likelihood of passable roads more probable. From what he could tell, the major highways in China were as good as those in the US. Massive amounts of commodities traveled thousands of kilometers every day by truck. One small vegetable delivery truck would hardly garner much notice.

The truck Cheng had given them told Ben that the vampire who'd loaned it was either a very good smuggler or a very real businessman. Possibly both. More of a delivery truck than a semi-rig, it was small enough that Ben would be able to drive it, big enough to hide the crates that Tenzin said they'd need, and just banged up enough to look like every other truck on the road. No fancy logos decorated the outside, but a very official set of characters and numbers were visible on the back.

He saw Tenzin frowning at the papers the vampire handed her. Would she know what to look for? He'd called Caspar earlier to double-check the research he'd done online. He knew there should be a forged commercial license for him, along with several different permits for each province they'd have to pass through. The paperwork made Ben nervous. There was so much and Tenzin, for all her expertise, was complete and total crap at understanding paperwork. Ignoring her earlier instructions, he walked over.

He spoke in Latin this time. "What is it?"

He held out his hand for the papers, and with an amused look, she handed them to him. They were all in Mandarin.

Of course they were. Shit.

Speaking Chinese was one thing. Reading and writing was completely different. And Ben's reading definitely qualified as "appalling."

Tenzin barely glanced at him, but continued talking with the other vampire, who held out an envelope. It looked like linen paper sealed in intricate fashion, a distinctive stamp pressed into rich red wax on both sides with a small jade bead making up the center of the stamp. Tenzin glanced at it, then put it in her pocket.

Cheng's man fired off rapid Mandarin that Ben had a hard time following. He thought the vampire was offering to hire them a driver—for a small extra fee, of course—but Tenzin immediately held up a hand.

"No, no, no," she said, more slowly. "I prefer my own driver."

"You don't trust Cheng?" There was a gleam in the vampire's eye. "I'm sure he would prefer his own driver for the truck. A gesture of consideration, of course."

Tenzin's mouth curled up in the corners, her eyes warmed, and Ben had to keep his mouth from dropping open.

It was the most unabashedly seductive smile he'd ever seen on her face.

"Oh, Cheng knows *exactly* how much I trust him. And so do you, Kesan."

Ben recognized the tone of her voice, he'd just never heard it from *her*.

But that smile was unmistakable, and now Ben wondered just who Cheng was to Tenzin.

He didn't think of that part of her life. Or the lack of it. He'd known she'd been mated to Beatrice's father, but it had been a political marriage. Wasn't it? He'd never seen her with a lover. Never seen her even show any interest in a man. Or a woman. Not with that kind of smile on her face.

Her body language still telling a story he wasn't sure he wanted to hear, Tenzin said, "Tell Cheng not to worry. If we have problems, he can be sure I will have my human get in touch with Jonathan."

His heartbeat had picked up, and he saw Tenzin's head angle toward him. She'd heard it, which meant the other vampire had, too.

Ben cursed himself silently. Any unexpected change in his pulse was something he'd been trained to control since he was a boy. Vampires may seem like genteel creatures, but at the heart, his aunt and uncle had never let him forget they were predators.

And predators chased prey.

"Do not become prey, Benjamin. Because if you do, you will be chased. And you will be caught."

His heartbeat was marking him as prey, and there was no way of explaining his unconscious reaction. Because it wasn't from fear. Fear was something he'd trained away for many years. It was from something far more complicated.

Tenzin's eyes met his for a moment, but he couldn't read their expression. It was dark and fleeting. Then her smile curved again, but it was false. Something inside him screamed and beat at the facade. Tenzin stepped closer and placed a hand on his cheek, rubbing her thumb under his lower lip absently. His pulse spiked again.

"Go wait for me in the truck," she said in soft English. "We'll only be a minute."

He pulled away from her and walked to the delivery truck, not understanding exactly what had happened. He climbed into the driver's seat and slid it back, surprised the Cheng's vampire had even fit in the truck to drive. Then he sat back and stared at the dashboard while his thoughts raced.

Tenzin and Cheng? Who was Jonathan?

Why the hell had she smiled at him like that, and why did the falseness of it grate against his nerves?

Tenzin and *Cheng*?

"He owes me a number of favors..."

Now Ben was wondering what kind of favors they traded.

He shook his head. It didn't matter. It was none of his business. But he couldn't forget her smile.

IT was more like an hour, and not the minute she promised, before Cheng's associate opened the truck door for Tenzin. She didn't hesitate as he'd seen her do with vehicles in the past. She lifted herself into the cab and settled on the passenger seat.

"I will see you in Shanghai, Kesan."

"Are you sure I cannot send my driver with you?"

"Quite sure."

"Safe travels. We will see you in the city."

Then the door was closed and Ben didn't have time to wonder at her ease getting into the truck. He started the engine and pulled away, pretending to be the professional he was supposed to be. Pretending not to notice the stiff set of her shoulders beside him.

They made it all of five blocks before she said, "Pull over."

He pulled over.

"What the hell was that?"

Now *that* tone was familiar.

He put the truck in park and sat back, but didn't turn to her.

"Explain yourself, Benjamin."

He shrugged.

"I had specific instructions before we left the hotel. Stay back. You're a driver. Not important. Don't make yourself visible."

"I know."

"But you just couldn't help yourself, could you?"

He said nothing. She was right. Even though it grated at the adolescent pride he knew was a weakness, he should have followed her instructions and made himself as inconspicuous as possible.

"Now you are visible. A person, not just a human who belongs to me. Kesan knows you are not only a driver. You are a driver who speaks Latin. Which he might speak, by the way, as Cheng's first is a former English clergyman. He also knows you speak Mandarin, because of the way you reacted to what I said about Cheng. What were you *thinking*?"

He hadn't been thinking. Clearly.

"I don't know."

"You don't? Because your heartbeat told Kesan that you were either frightened, angry, or reacting to something else. Frightened and angry are the worse options, so now, he thinks I've brought my young lover to China into the territory of his master, who has never been known to share well with others."

"And what, exactly, would he be sharing?" Ben muttered.

She was on him in a heartbeat. Clutching his chin to

force his face to her as she bared her fangs.

"Your presumption irritates me. Do not forget who I am, Benjamin Vecchio."

Ben stared at her, unblinking, and his pulse didn't trip. It had been a long time since he'd seen her this angry. He took a deep breath and opened his mouth, but she cut him off before he could speak, jerking his chin to the side as she sat back in her own seat. He could still feel the edges of her nails in his neck.

"I don't want to hear your explanation. I expected better from you. You're too smart to act this stupid, Ben. Don't let it happen again. For now, we play things as they stand."

"And how do they stand?" he asked, putting the truck back into gear.

"Cheng will dismiss you. He pays little attention to any humans. That is what Jonathan is for."

"Jealous former boyfriend, huh?" He tried to control the flush of anger he could feel on his cheeks, but knew she probably scented his blood rising.

"Boyfriend is a ridiculous human term for the three hundred year old water vampire who controls the Shanghai Group. And what Cheng is to me is none of your business. Drive."

HE didn't say another word until they got back to the hotel. Then, it was terse questions and quick answers. Weapons were packed. Supplies were stowed. He checked out, even though they only had a few hours of driving before dawn. It would be enough to start out of the city; Ben only hoped they could find daylight shelter along the road.

An hour after they'd left the lights of Ürümqi behind, he asked her, "What are you going to do during the day?"

"I think the safest route is to stay in the back of the truck. Find a petrol station or a way station where you can rest. If you sleep in the front, no one will look in the back. I won't sleep anyway, so as long as I stay out of the light, I'll be fine."

"Is there a vent back there?"

"I'll be fine, Ben."

He didn't like the idea of her being trapped in the back of the truck, but then, he pitied anyone who tried to break in. Tenzin was still dangerous, even at noon. The truck came equipped with curtains for the front windows, so he'd be able to sleep on the bench in relative privacy. It was probably a better plan than trying to find a hotel or some other lodging on the road.

"Fine," he said. "I'll look for a rest stop once it starts to get light. I'm getting pretty tired."

He'd had a total of six hours of sleep in the past twenty four hours. Not the worst he'd ever clocked, but not ideal, especially when he was navigating foreign roads in a truck he'd never driven before. One hundred fifty kilometers out of Ürümqi, he was feeling it, and he could see the sky starting to lighten.

"Next place," Tenzin murmured. She'd been silent for most of the trip. Usually, when they were together, it was a nonstop back and forth of jokes and stories. Now...

"I'm sorry," he said, spotting a sign for what looked like a travel plaza. Two truck in front of him were exiting the highway, so he followed them.

"About what?"

"About earlier. I was trying to help, but I know I messed things up."

Her voice was slightly warmer when she answered. "This can be a very dangerous place. I'm trying to protect you."

"I know."

"It would be easier if you were vampire."

"Not gonna happen," he whispered.

"You're too young to make that decision."

It was an old argument. One he'd been having off and on with her since he was seventeen. One he didn't feel like having at the moment, so he let it drop.

Ben pulled off the road and found a place to park among the other trucks at the road stop. His was not the only delivery truck on the lot, though most were the larger diesel trucks that filled the highway. Still, they were in Xinjiang, so the mix of faces was diverse enough to warrant no second looks when he went in to use the bathroom and grab a bowl of noodles to fill his stomach. There were truckers there, but also many other travelers. Even a Westerner with a small group of Han Chinese, who looked like they were dressed for business.

No one spared him a glance.

He made it back to the truck and handed Tenzin the tea he'd bought for her.

She was grinning. "Look what I found."

He took a long drink of water and climbed in the truck. "What's up?"

"Cheng's people are quite clever. That is what is up."

She tugged the curtains closed and pulled away the back cushion on the passenger's side, revealing a hatch about the size of a large dog door.

"What is that?"

"I checked in the cargo area, but you can't see it from there. A false wall! It's been welded in place. You can't access it from the compartment, only from the driver's area."

"A smuggler's hatch? Nice."

She shrugged. "It's always good to have some places that remain invisible from prying eyes."

"Will the crates fit in there?"

She shook her head. "It's about the width of a twin bed, if not narrower. And only accessed by this door. You could fit something small, but it's made for hiding a person."

"Or persons," he said grimly, knowing that more than one vampire was involved in human trafficking.

Of course, a lot of humans were involved in that, too.

"Cheng quit that business many years ago. He does still move some people discreetly, but only those who want to be moved."

He didn't really want to hear about Cheng.

"It'll be a perfect resting place for you," he said, "as long as you don't mind crawling inside."

It was pretty small, but then, so was Tenzin. She grinned and handed him her cup of tea, then slipped through with the practiced ease of a cat burglar.

"Comfortable in there?"

"It's cozy." She stuck her head through and he handed her the tea. "There is a fan. It's well ventilated. Completely light proof."

"Good." He knew she could take care of herself, but he still hadn't liked the idea of her in the more easily accessed back while he was sleeping. "Escape routes?"

She pulled back, and he heard her shuffling around. "One in the floor and... if I had to, I could punch out the welds on this wall. They're not solid."

"Of course they aren't," he muttered. "You do realize that this is Cheng's truck. He knows that compartment is there."

"I don't sleep, Benjamin." She stuck her head through the hatch. "I'm hardly vulnerable during the nighttime, and I'm not worried about humans during the day."

"No?"

"Cheng doesn't trust anyone who can be manipulated by *amnis*."

"Ah." *Please don't get chatty about Cheng.*

She disappeared back into her bolt-hole. Ben locked the truck doors and cracked the windows, thankful that the air in the mountains was cool and dry. Stuffing a duffel bag under his head, he stretched out as much as he could. His knees were bent, which he knew he'd pay for in the morning, but he didn't have many options.

"I may not trust Cheng," Tenzin continued in a muffled voice, "but he's still quite possessive. He might try to kill me, but he wouldn't let anyone else do it in his territory."

"Sounds like a lovely relationship." He kept his eyes closed and mentally begged her to shut up.

"Relationship is not a way I would describe it."

I don't want to know, he mouthed silently.

"It's been years since I've seen him."

"Goodnight, Tenzin."

"Goodnight." She reached through the hatch and squeezed his hand. The spark of *amnis* was unmistakable.

"Tenzin did you—"

"You need to rest." Her voice was muffled by the steel compartment and the fog of sleep that was quickly descending.

"Tiny, I..."

The world around him turned feather soft.

He heard her whisper, "I would have you rest easy, my Benjamin."

It was the last thing he heard before he fell into a deep and dreamless sleep.

Chapter Five

DESPITE BEN'S FEARS, the two day drive to Kashgar was uneventful. Save for the near-constant griping of his travel companion, Ben almost found it relaxing.

"You are a terrible driver," she muttered as he took another hairpin turn.

"I'm not. I'm actually a very good driver." He *was* a good driver. He'd known how to drive a car since he was ten and though Gio had never allowed Beatrice to see them, he'd driven his uncle around long before he had a proper license.

He didn't really enjoy freaking her out. But the upside of Tenzin being a curled ball in the seat across from him was that she wasn't letting her curiosity get the better of her. This was a newer truck and vampire *amnis* would short out the dashboard if she tried to mess with it.

"You're going to make the truck crash."

He laughed. "You're funny."

"No, I'm not. I'm..."

"You're what?" He chanced a glance over, only to see her sitting precariously in the seat, lifting herself in the air every time they went over a bump, clutching the small handle over the door. Her face was still and her teeth were clenched.

"You're scared," he said, shocked by the sudden realization. Tenzin wasn't scared of anything. Not really. She was often cautious, but scared?

"Do you realize how utterly defenseless you are in this

vehicle? It is not a van, it is a giant trap."

"How many exits?" It was a game they often played. Tenzin asking him how many ways out of a room or random location. Ben quickly giving her all the available exits, with her usually adding one or two more.

Tenzin said nothing.

"Come on, Tiny. How many exits?"

"None!"

"Wrong. Kick out the front window. One. Break open the side doors. Two and Three. Moon roof." He rapped on the overhead hatch. "Four. In this small a room, four exits is more than enough."

Tenzin glanced speculatively at the moonroof. "It opens?"

He put a hand up and popped it up. It wasn't automatic, but the plastic joints gave easily, allowing a quick suck of air into the cab. He could see Tenzin relax almost immediately.

"Four," she said. "That is sufficient."

"More than sufficient. After all," he said, flicking his eyes toward the now-easy vampire, "you really only need one."

"I wouldn't leave you behind if we fell over a cliff," she said, neck craning to look over the edge of the road through the mountains.

"That's comforting."

"Unless it was you who drove us over the cliff. Then you'd deserve it."

"I'll keep that in mind."

ANOTHER city, another eerily quiet warehouse.

Someday, Ben would write a book—probably a very short book—on how universal most cities were. Yes, they all had their quirks, but on the whole, he found them to be startlingly similar. Smells changed the most. This time, when they opened the door, the earthy smell of vegetables met their nose. Ben could see crates stacked on one wall of the warehouse Tenzin directed him toward. He'd pulled into the warehouse and barely stopped before Tenzin burst out of the vehicle, flying up to the rafters of the warehouse and perching there like a very large bird.

"Tenzin?"

"Just let me sit up here for a while."

"Take your time." He went to close the giant door of the warehouse. Light was sucked out of the room as the door rolled closed, but he could hear Tenzin fluttering in the rafters as she stretched her legs.

"You're going to have to find lodgings," she said. "There's not enough time to start tonight. Cheng's man said there is a motorbike in the warehouse somewhere."

He stood, looking up at her and frowning. "So you want me to just run out and find a hotel—"

"Not a hotel. Anyone local will be watching hotels." Her dark eyebrows furrowed together. "What do you call the place where the backpackers sleep?"

"A tent?"

"No, where they go when they're not camping."

"A hostel?"

"Yes." She smiled. "Use one of those. There are probably several, and they are less likely to be watched. Find one near the old city."

"But don't you—"

"I'll stay here," she said. "Plenty of room to fly and the

windows have been blacked out."

"Are you sure?" He couldn't see a thing in the warehouse. There was a small light over the door, but once he'd rolled down the door, the space had been plunged into darkness. He had no idea how he was going to find this motorbike Cheng's man had mentioned if he couldn't even—

He tripped over something in the darkness, smashing his shin.

"Ow," he said through gritted teeth.

"Found the bike?"

"Yes." More like, the bike had found him. And it wasn't a bike. It was a scooter. "Tenzin, I don't like the idea of leaving you here."

She found a light near another door and flicked it on. It wasn't much, but it was enough to illuminate the warehouse with a grey light.

"Why not?" she asked. "There is plenty of room to kill anyone who comes after me and you need a bath." She flew down in front of him, her nose slightly wrinkled. "Really. A bath. At once."

He pushed a hand through her tangled mop of hair. "You're looking lovely, too, my delicate Himalayan flower."

Tenzin laughed, the full-bodied burst of sound he loved to hear.

"Okay," Ben said. "I'll go out and find something. I have my phone."

"No hotels."

"No hotels." It looked like there were a few hostels in the old part of the city. "I'll manage. The scooter is mine?"

"Yours. Try not to drive it off a cliff."

"Did I get us here in one piece?" He threw a backpack

over his shoulder. It was packed with a change of clothes and a few other essentials. Good thing he traveled light, since his suitcase wasn't going to fit on the rickety old Vespa. "Where do you want to meet tomorrow night?"

"I'll find you," she said. "Get some sleep."

The thought of stretching out, even on a hard Chinese mattress, was appealing. He gave Tenzin a quick nod, then pushed the scooter out the door, into the familiar unfamiliarity of Kashgar at four in the morning. A quick look at the map on his phone, and he was off.

TENZIN watched him go, amused by Benjamin's ease on the bike. In the city. Everywhere.

He was an easy travel companion, one she didn't have to worry about taking care of himself. A chameleon who slid into any situation with ease, he was as comfortable in a back alley bar as he was in a five star restaurant. Giovanni had given him part of that, but much of it was simply Ben himself. And though the young man avoided troublesome situations with the caution of a hardened street child, he now had the body and skills of a warrior. Years of training had seen to that.

His reaction to Cheng had been... odd. She couldn't decide if it would be problematic yet, so she didn't spend much mental energy on it. Nevertheless, he had made himself notable, and Kesan would be sure to mention his presence to Jonathan, if not to Cheng himself. Tenzin didn't often travel with humans, so they would tuck the knowledge away, possibly for use at a later time.

Whether Ben drew more attention to himself beyond a passing notice would be something they would have to discuss. Cheng had a habit of considering Tenzin "his" when she was in his presence, and Ben needed to be able to ignore it. Had he been surprised by the idea of her having past lovers? That was amusing. She was five thousand years old. A practical vampire. Lovers could be an excellent way to pass time. She was choosy and discreet, but by no means did she ignore that part of her life anymore.

Tenzin had Cheng to thank for some of that. It was the reason he was allowed his presumption of claiming her. Cheng knew he was audacious, but he winked and smiled his thief's smile. Then she would laugh and allow him to steal her for a time.

Tenzin enjoyed his boldness, though even her amusement had limits. Their intimate relationship was mostly in the past, though Cheng had been more than open about his willingness to rekindle it if she ever desired. She'd never known whether his interest was political or personal. It was probably both, and she could hardly blame him. The canny immortal leader was well aware of her status at Penglai Island, and had more than once flaunted their relationship to tweak her sire. Cheng enjoyed rubbing his success and newly amassed power in the face of the Elders. They were everything old about China, and he was everything new. He reveled in their annoyance.

It was that energy and ambition that had attracted her in the first place. Cheng was so very alive. And when they had been together, Tenzin allowed herself to feel the same way. It was Cheng she'd fled to after Stephen had died. Cheng who had welcomed her black presence and asked no questions, no matter how many crowded his eyes.

Yes, her gratitude to the pirate extended rather far.

How long had it been since she'd taken a lover? Certainly not in the time she'd been in Los Angeles.

Perhaps Ben *had* been surprised.

No matter. He would have to conquer his own reactions, though the fiction she'd created for Kesan would do for now to explain any odd responses the young man continued to have. Ben being her human paramour was a useful lie, so they'd continue it while they were in China, even though the necessity of it annoyed her.

Tenzin wasn't ready for Benjamin to make himself notable yet.

That would come in time. Like Giovanni, he would have to make himself feared if he wanted to live in any kind of peace in their world. But though he was young, she had seen the flashes in his eyes. Seen the grim determination against an opponent. He would never be a man to seek out violence, but he did not shrink from it. He had killed his first man when he was only sixteen. Killed the human in defense of a friend. An honorable first kill. Tenzin held his hand when he grieved his loss of innocence.

He'd only shed tears once.

Benjamin Vecchio would be a formidable immortal. This ridiculous need to cling to his humanity annoyed her.

She spoke her will into the still night air. "He is young. We will change his mind."

BEN stretched out on the bed, which he'd dragged to the window overlooking the street. He propped the blinds open and listened to the morning call to prayer as it echoed down the narrow street in the old city. Though part of the new reconstruction, the neighborhood still held the flavor of the mud houses he'd seen on the road into town. So much of the old city was being demolished to widen roads and create safer housing. He hoped the character of this unique place could remain, because he already loved it.

It smelled of dust and roasted mutton. Bread and sesame hung in the early morning air. He closed his eyes against the grey light and took a deep breath. The tentative morning sounds started when the call to prayer died down.

As the city started to wake, he dozed.

He'd woken the young Chinese man who ran the hostel with a friend, begging a place to stay for a few days and offering enough yuan to make it worth his time. It was a hostel, but Ben had a private room and a bath, so he couldn't complain. It was basic, but comfortable. And the quiet courtyard outside his room was lined with low tables and rugs. A comfortable place to remain anonymous.

Plus, you could never complain about free wifi.

He closed his eyes and dropped off to sleep. When he woke, it was already dark, and Tenzin sat in the window, perched on the wide ledge. He wondered if she'd flown up to it and if anyone had seen her. She made a picture, sitting there, her tangled braids wild from the wind. Black tunic and leggings. She was darkness in vampire form, her face the pale moon against the black night of her hair.

Ben reached under his pillow and grabbed his phone, snapping a picture of her before she could object.

"Don't."

"Too late." He hid the phone under the sheet that covered him from the waist down. "Did you fly?" he asked, his voice rasping with sleep.

She shook her head. “Dropped from the roof. The roofs here are wonderful. Very easy to run across. If they don’t fall in when you land on them.”

“I’ll keep that in mind.”

“Just avoid the older ones,” she said. “You were tired.”

He stretched up his arms, then absently scratched the line of hair that ran down the center of his stomach. “Exhausted.”

Tenzin cocked her head. “You have grown so tall. I forget sometimes that you cannot curl up as I can. The truck must have been uncomfortable.”

“It was fine. I’m not that tall.”

“Far taller than me.”

He was. But then, Tenzin was barely five foot.

“What’s the plan?” He grabbed his shirt from the floor by the bed where he’d dropped it and held it to his nose before he grimaced. Nope. Wasn’t going to get another day out of that one. The drizzle of a shower last night had cleaned his body, but his clothes were another matter. There were clothes lines in the courtyard, but he didn’t know if he had time to do laundry.

“We can walk to the house from here. We’ll have to sneak into the old town. Only residents are supposed to go in there.”

“Is it that dangerous?”

She shrugged. “I don’t know. We’ll see. There’s no question it will be demolished when the government finally gets to it, and the cache is buried beneath a house. It must be moved. There is no telling what the condition of anything will be.”

He rubbed his eyes and started to think practically.

"Transportation?"

"We won't be able to get a truck in, but we might be able to pay some locals to help us. Hand carts and the like."

Ben shook his head. "Nothing goes without one of us accompanying it. You saw the crates in back of the truck. What's your estimate?"

"To pack everything?" She mulled it over. "I think... ten. They can't be too heavy because we'll have to carry them."

"That's it?"

Tenzin grinned. "The most valuable things are often the smallest. Size is no guarantee of quality."

He left that one alone. She probably wouldn't get the joke anyway.

"Okay, so we could carry things out with a large cart. I'm guessing small, but heavy. How far to a main road?"

"Not far. A few blocks only. I'll find a driver and... persuade him to stay with the truck while we're loading everything up."

"Persuade" likely meant she'd brainwash one with *amnis*. He didn't have the inclination to argue. To accomplish this, they'd need all vampire tricks available.

"Okay, so tonight we'll—"

"Grab the crates from the warehouse."

"We crate up the gold," Ben said, "then haul it to the truck."

Tenzin nodded. "I'll stay with the truck through the day. You stay here and enjoy a human-sized bed as long as you can. We can leave tomorrow night."

"Fair enough." There was something he wasn't... Damn it, why did she always have to hit him with stuff when he was sleepy or distracted? She did that shit on purpose.

"It's settled." She leaned toward the street. "I'll give you a few minutes to—"

"Wait!" He rubbed his eyes, wracking his brain for the tail of the problem he'd detected. There was something...

"Anyone local will be watching hotels..."

"Tenzin, who's the VIC here?" It was his own shorthand for Vampire In Charge. Because there was *always* a vampire in charge. Some areas had quiet vamps, who looked the other way on pretty much anything. Other areas had micromanagers. But if there were people and resources, there was a VIC. And Ben had a feeling this far west, it wasn't Cheng.

"Tenzin?"

She pursed her lips.

"Tell me it's not someone who hates you."

"This is slightly embarrassing."

"Why?"

"Because I don't know who is in charge here."

"You don't?" That was surprising, considering her memory.

"In this area, it's almost constantly changing. Power struggles are a way of life."

"Why didn't you ask Kesan?"

She looked offended. "And let him know that I do not know who runs this area? Hardly."

"So, rather than look bad in front of someone you mildly trust, you're going into a city and taking out gold when you have no idea who the VIC is *at all*?"

She shrugged. "It's my gold."

"They may not see it that way, since it's been in their

territory for over two hundred years, Tenzin."

"No matter. I hardly think we'll arouse any interest."

"Really? You're so full of shit."

She smiled.

Ben groaned. "You're itching for a fight, aren't you?"

"It's been a while."

He sat up and grabbed for his backpack, rifling through to find a clean shirt.

"Fine. Whatever. Don't get me killed and remember the golden rule of pissing VICs off."

"I have no idea what you're talking about."

He leaned forward and grabbed her chin between his fingers, forcing her to look at him. "You break it, you buy it. So unless you want to be the de facto immortal leader of a small city in Central Asia, don't kill anyone, Tenzin."

She pouted. "You really like spoiling a fight, don't you? And this is faulty reasoning. If they try to hurt us, I'm going to kill them. I don't care what happens afterward."

"Why do I even bother?" He went back to his backpack. Yeah, he was definitely going to have to do laundry. "Fine. Try not to kill anyone important."

"Of course."

"Happy now?"

"Always." She leaned over and rolled onto his bed, shoving him toward the edge. "Oh, this *is* comfortable. I'll just wait here while you get dressed."

"Boundary issues, Tenzin."

"What?"

He shook his head and walked to the tiny bathroom, hoping he wouldn't give himself a concussion trying to get dressed. "Nevermind."

Chapter Six

IT WAS INEVITABLE that everything went to hell the second he thought they were clear.

Ben and Tenzin had made their way to one of the oldest crumbling neighborhoods of Kashgar around midnight, the moon full enough to give them some light, which was good because street lamps weren't something the city had invested in for this part of town. Most of the light came from open doors and a few windows. Many of the houses were already deserted. Mud brick walls lined the narrow streets as they turned and twisted further into the dark maze of square houses.

Eventually, they came to a crumbling wooden gate. Tenzin paused, putting her finger to her lips. She listened for a few minutes. Then, without turning to Ben, she leapt into the air and over the wall. He heard a few steps. A pause. More steps. He was reaching for the door handles when the gate suddenly swung open on squeaky hinges. Ben immediately pulled out the small can of spray lubricant he'd picked up that day to quiet the gate.

"Sorry," Tenzin said. "Needed to make sure we were alone. The family is gone."

"Gone?" His eyes swept the bare courtyard. Though the gate had been in bad shape, the courtyard was neat and relatively intact. Three houses opened onto it, all two story with carved wooden beams supporting the bricks.

Numerous windows showed that, at one time, the houses had been showpieces. A covered cistern was in the center of the courtyard and brick planters lined the walls. But all the plants in them were dead. Old vines had fallen over and not even a bird or a rat lingered.

"I don't like this," Ben said.

"I don't know if they'd been paid since Nima died. It's possible they just moved on."

"You have got to get someone hired to take care of your paperwork, Tiny."

She shrugged.

Ben shook his head. "You think your cache is still here?"

"We'll see, won't we?"

Without another word, she walked over to the cistern and pulled open the grate.

"You stored it in a cistern? I thought you said—"

"There is a false wall. I borrowed an earth vampire to dig it so that the water would run to one side while keeping my things dry on the other. He did an excellent job. This area doesn't get enough rain to be a danger." She slipped inside, her narrow body disappearing beneath the earth. Ben tried not to shiver.

"You used an earth vampire to dig it?"

"Yes." Her voice echoed up from below.

"How did you know he wouldn't come back and steal from you?"

There was no sound for a few minutes, and then Ben heard a smashing. Then a crumbling, as if rocks were tumbling down. He wondered if Tenzin would answer his question or just let him wonder. Finally, her dusty face peeked through the hole, hovering just under the surface.

"He wasn't a very nice earth vampire."

"Oh."

She smiled. "It looks like everything is still here. The question is, do you want to start sorting or get the crates?"

"Is there a ladder?"

"Not down here."

He spun around and saw one leaning on the second floor of one of the houses, propped against the roof. Ben walked over and stood at the doorway of the empty house, pausing to listen for any traces of occupation. There was nothing, so he went inside.

Flicking on the flashlight he'd pocketed, he could see it was definitely empty. Dust and a few broken pieces of furniture were all that was left. He made his way up the stairs, a few bits of straw and mud falling as he climbed.

Maybe it was being raised in earthquake-prone California, but Ben shuddered at the thought of living there. The whole place felt like it was about to crumble. He found his way to the walkway that ran around the outside of the second story and found the ladder, carefully lowering into Tenzin's waiting hands in the courtyard below.

"You go get the crates," he whispered. "I'll start sorting."

She nodded and took off into the night, the dark flap of her black tunic sounding more like a night bird than a person. She kept to the shadows, hopping along the roofs of the houses until she was out of sight.

Ben climbed back down to the courtyard, relieved that the ladder seemed to hold his weight, then he lowered the thing into the cistern and took a deep breath.

"Please no rats," he whispered. "Or snakes."

HOLY SHIT.

He'd watched movies. Seen some pretty amazing museum exhibits. But nothing really compared to holding a really large bar of pure gold in your hand.

Holy shit.

It was heavier than he'd expected. Really heavy. The small bars were nothing like the bullion he'd seen pictures of at Fort Knox. No, these were closer to the size of a deck of cards, with just a little more length. There was a symbol he couldn't read pressed into them and pieces had been sliced or chopped off here and there, so they were far from uniform.

Still, that much gold in one place… And this was only *one* of her caches.

The gold bars had been stored in small wooden boxes, crumbled by the inevitable passing of years. Silks, old tapestries, and carpets were piled on top of the boxes, but most of those were molded or moth-eaten. He removed them carefully, placing them in one corner of the small room half the size of his walk-in closet at home. There were a few pieces Tenzin might want to save. Other than that, there were two boxes of remarkably intact porcelain packed in moldy straw, one box that looked like it contained idols of different kinds, and another small box he'd saved for last.

"Oh yeah," he whispered, guessing the small chest was where Tenzin had placed the jewelry she'd mentioned. It was locked, so he took out the set of picks he always carried with him and eased the old latch open, touching the rusted joints with the oil he'd brought. "Come on…"

A click. A crack. And there it was. The lid swung up.

"Hello, beautiful."

There was a jumble of gold chains and loose stones in the bottom of the box. He saw a ruby almost the size of his thumb. A twisted diadem of some kind. A gold and garnet crown. Earrings, most of them pressed and engraved gold. Chains and bracelets of every thickness and length were tangled in the bottom of the box.

And then there was the necklace.

It was a thick crescent of pure gold that would fit around a woman's neck with a delicate series of chains hanging in back. Tiny twisting depictions of animals with hunters following them in chariots. Flowers and mythical figures he thought were probably griffins. He tried to date it, but he couldn't. He'd have to look it up. It wasn't Egyptian or Greek.

He was going to have to do a lot more reading if he was going to treasure hunt with Tenzin.

"Scythian," came a whisper over his shoulder.

Ben spun to see Tenzin hovering over him with a grin. "You're going to have to work on that. Anyone could have snuck in and knocked you over the head while you were mooning over that necklace. Don't get gold-dumb."

"Sorry." He held the necklace up. "This one. This is the piece I want."

She cocked an eyebrow. "Just like that? You should ask me what the provenance is. Where I found it. Or stole it."

"I don't really care," he admitted. "I want it."

"As I said, it's Scythian. Third or fourth century. Closer to fourth, I think. I found it in Russia."

"Is it mine?"

She looked around the room. “As soon as we get these packed and out of here, yes. I’m assuming you want to keep it with the the rest of the treasure for now.”

Tenzin held out her hand and waited.

With effort, Ben held out the necklace, which was already warm from his hands.

“Don’t be greedy,” she whispered. “It’s been around for sixteen hundred years. It’s not going to disappear.”

He handed it over.

“You have very good taste, by the way,” Tenzin said. “This is one of the best pieces in this cache. If I was trading, I’d ask for at least two of these gold bars in exchange.”

“Why? It’s not half as heavy as one of the bars.”

“But the craftsmanship.” She trailed her fingers over a line of flowers that decorated the top loop of the crescent. “Keep this one. It’s a good piece. An auspicious start to your own collection. I took it in trade from a man I respected a great deal. I’ll tell you the story someday.” She put it back in the box, examining the open lock with a smile. “But not now. Let’s get to work. You climb up and I’ll hand you the pieces.”

He walked to the ladder as Tenzin bent near the rugs and the silks.

“Have you ever lost things?” he asked.

“Lost? No.” She picked up one silk carpet that was only ragged on one edge. “I always find things eventually. Had things stolen? Yes.”

“Who stole from you?”

“Remember that earth vampire I mentioned?”

“Oh.”

She looked up. “I left him in his element.”

Realizing she must have killed the vampire and left his body to disintegrate down in the cistern, he cringed.

"Ew."

She shrugged and went back to sorting through the pile. "Dust to dust. One day, I will be air. Dissolve into nothing more than a drift on the breeze."

"No," he said, not wanting to think about a world without Tenzin. "Forget the breeze, Tiny. We all know you'd be a hurricane."

She laughed quietly, her eyes sparkling in the low glimmer of the flashlight he'd propped in the corner.

"I'll go up and start," Ben said. "It's going to be a long night."

IT was hot dusty work, even if you were a vampire. Tenzin had a seemingly endless supply of energy, flying back and forth from the bottom to the mouth of the cistern, handing up a few rugs, porcelain bowls and vases, and brick after brick of gold. They worked silently for three hours until the majority of the cache was packed.

Ben distributed the gold evenly between ten crates so none would be too heavy to carry. He'd found a hand cart that afternoon, so while Tenzin sorted through the last of the silks and porcelain, he went to get it from the truck, glad he'd remembered to bring the chalk he used for caving. He marked the path through the old neighborhood with surreptitious white tags at waist level, which allowed him to walk through the maze of old houses and back to the truck with ease. He retrieved the handcart and started back to the courtyard where Tenzin was finishing up.

He drew a few curious glances from windows, but it

was three in the morning and most of the old city was asleep. Very few lights illuminated the alleyways or houses. Ben felt utterly alone. Alone was good. When you were transporting a bunch of priceless treasure, company was not a desirable thing.

The city was quiet. So quiet that, when he turned the last corner, the sound of shuffling feet in the courtyard brought him up short. Tenzin didn't shuffle. Mostly, she floated.

Shit.

Ben didn't hear her, but he did hear strange male voices speaking Uyghur. Someone was in the courtyard and he could hear them opening the crates he'd just nailed shut.

Bastards.

They laughed softly, then he heard one kick something metal. Then came the sound of wood breaking, and Ben knew they'd broken the ladder. More sound of metal on bricks, and he realized the heavy plate would be back over the cistern, trapping Tenzin under the earth.

Not good.

He peeked through the cracked gate and saw three vampires poking through the contents of the crates. One held up a vase as another dug through the straw.

"You're poking through her stuff and tried to trap her underground," he murmured. "You must really want to die."

THE moment the grate fell over the opening of the cistern, the shot of instinctive panic streaked through Tenzin. She could feel the press of the narrow walls around her and, for just a second, the taste of earth was in her mouth.

Tenzin hated being underground.

She narrowed her eyes and eyed the lovely little treasure she'd just unearthed from the tangle of a crumbling tapestry.

It was a bone-handled *pesh-kabz*, a Persian blade she'd picked up in the eighteenth century from a trader on the Khyber Pass. Lovely. Still in excellent condition. And more than capable of taking care of the foolish vampires who'd tried to trap her.

Tenzin floated to the top of the cistern, peeking through the grate to see who was examining her gold.

Where was Ben? Hopefully, by the time he got back with the handcart, she'd have hidden all the bodies. He did get strangely upset when she had to kill people, even if they were vampires.

One of them was muttering and holding out a brick of gold with her mark on it. If they had any sense, they'd realize who it belonged to, drop it back in the crate, and run. If they did, she'd let them live. After all, she was done with this hiding place anyway.

The vampire showed the mark to the one who seems to be in charge. He cocked his head like a spaniel, shrugged, and grabbed the brick, slipping it into his pocket.

Obviously, they were idiots and she was going to have to kill them. Vampires that stupid just made the rest of their race look bad.

SHOULD he go in? Wait outside? Ben was fairly sure Tenzin didn't need any help, and she might even get annoyed it he tried. It wasn't as if the metal grate was that heavy. Maybe the vampires didn't realize she could fly. While Ben debated how much carnage he wanted to witness, he saw the grate begin to move. While one vampire halted what he was doing to look at it, the others had disappeared from his sight.

Oh shit.

They ripped the door from its hinges and pulled Ben into the courtyard. He wasted no time, years of practice kicking in. It was all automatic reaction. As they tossed him into the air, he tucked and rolled, reaching down to the small sheathes strapped to his ankles. Pulling out his throwing knives as he landed, he immediately aimed at the nearest vampire, who was still coming forward, laughing at the silly human they'd caught.

The vampire's scream when the knife caught his eye shattered the moon-lit night. He pulled at the knife, covering his bleeding eye with one hand, while the other curled into a fist. The bloody immortal bared his fangs and charged him, but tripped over a crate as he clutched his face. Ben could see the grate sliding open from the corner of his eye. Like a shadow, Tenzin rose from the earth, grabbing the vampire nearest the cistern by the hair. She cut his throat before he could make a sound. Then, still holding his head as the blood poured down his front, she drew back the dagger and hacked at the vampire's spine. With two heavy thwacks, the body dropped.

The vampire with two eyes rushed to Ben, crouching over him, his fangs almost in Ben's neck before Ben was able to bring his knife up. He forced the blade under the vampire's ribs just as a flying head collided with his attacker's temple, blood and brain matter spattering the bricks as the vampire released Ben.

Ben spit something he didn't want to think about out of his mouth as he rolled to his back, bringing his legs up and punching them into the torso of the vampire still on top of him. The kick drove the dagger in deeper. It caught in the immortal's ribs, and Ben heard a soft crack.

The two vampires were still shouting. Then it was only one. Ben's head whipped around to see the vampire with the bloody eye in a heap on the bricks. This time, it took three thwacks to decapitate him.

Ben felt his stomach lurch.

Then it was done and only one was left. Tenzin walked over, her blood-drenched tunic flapping as she approached him.

"Are you injured?"

"No. Just... trying not to puke."

Tenzin grabbed the last vampire by the hair, batting off the square hat the man wore and bringing up the dagger she held. "Ben, this is a good lesson on why you do not let your blades become dull. Obviously, it creates greater mess when you have to use them and can be to your detriment in a fight."

Don't throw up. Don't throw up.

"Got it, Tenzin."

Ben pulled off his bloody shirt and wiped his face, but he wasn't sure if it cleaned anything or just spread the blood around.

He didn't throw up.

Tenzin flew up, dragging the vampire to the balcony on the second floor of the house. Ben sure as hell hoped no one was looking over the wall, especially since there'd been so much noise. She sat on the edge of the balcony, kicking her legs back and forth and dangling the bloody stranger in front of her.

"Who is your master?" she asked in her most reasonable tone. She was using Mandarin and he wasn't sure why. Tenzin spoke Uyghur. Was it for his benefit?

"Are you going to kill me?"

"Yes. But I will kill you at a later time if you tell me who your master is."

"Eh..."

Obviously, this wasn't what the vampire wanted to hear.

Tenzin explained, "I am very old. So it's quite possible I'll forget about you for decades. Though I will kill you eventually."

"My sire is Aqpasha."

"Well," she said with a snort, "he thinks a lot of himself, doesn't he?"

"What?"

"Nevermind. I am Tenzin. Have you heard my name, even if you obviously haven't seen my mark?"

The vampire nodded.

"Then you know you should never try to take what is mine. Benjamin, there is a brick in one of the men's pockets, grab it please."

"Since you said please..." Ben muttered, rolling his shoulders and trying to ignore the bruises on his back he could feel forming.

"Now, vampire, what is your name—never mind, it is not important and you'll probably lie to me so I can't find you again." She pulled him closer and snarled, "It won't work. I have your smell. So tell me, did Aqpasha send you or were you exploring?"

He muttered something in Uyghur and Ben tuned out the conversation. After a few more pointed questions, she dropped him. The bloody vampire fell in the courtyard below, eyeing Ben with bitter eyes as he pulled out the knife still lodged in his ribs. Ben raised one eyebrow at the vampire as he threw the knife at Ben's feet.

"Pick the knife up, clean it, and hand it to my human," Tenzin called. She was examining the bodies of the other vampires, kicking them to the walls as their blood filled the cracks between the cobblestones, slowly creeping toward the cistern. She picked up Ben's other knife that had dropped near the crates and tossed it to him.

Ben caught it with a wince, slicing his finger open on the edge of the blade. "Careful, Tenzin."

The remaining vampire lunged toward the scent of Ben's blood, but before he could reach him, Tenzin tossed one of the severed heads at the vampire's ankles, tripping him as he tumbled at Ben's feet. Then she flew over, leaned down, and whispered in the man's ear before she cut his throat.

"I suppose it's later."

Chapter Seven

"WHEN ARE YOU going to start speaking to me again?" Tenzin asked, sitting uneasily across from Ben in the truck. It wasn't his anger making her uneasy. It was his driving. She was completely at ease with his anger.

Whatever.

"This is going to be a very long trip," she continued, "if you refuse to speak to me."

Ben said nothing. He was pissed. More than pissed. Actually angry. Because they'd killed three vampires who belonged to someone he assumed was important, they'd sped out of Kashgar as soon as the truck was loaded. They didn't go back to his hostel. They didn't see the Apak Hoja Mausoleum like he'd wanted to. They didn't get to visit the market or the central mosque. And all of his things, including his books, were left at the hostel. All he had on him was the bag with his computer, wallet, and passport. And his weapons.

Fucking Tenzin.

It wasn't the first time she'd pulled him into some shit she dreamed up or sought out. And while she'd saved his life, he was fairly convinced a little strong-arming and verbal intimidation of the VIC would have avoided the entire mess. But why find the vampire in charge and negotiate when you could just kill a bunch of people you didn't care about? And if your traveling companion had a little brain matter splattered across his face and had to knife someone in the gut, what was the big deal?

She settled into the seat across from him and Ben kept driving. By his calculation, they had a little over two hours of full night left. Then, Tenzin could crawl in the cubby hole for the rest of the trip, as far as he was concerned. He had half a mind to leave her in the middle of Xinjiang and fly home. Only the lure of the gold and garnet Scythian necklace carefully packed with the rest of her cache and surrounded by wilted vegetables made him stick with the truck.

Mercenary? Maybe. But then, he was traveling with a mercenary. Tenzin didn't lie about that. Why would she when she enjoyed it?

Ben glanced at her, but her eyes were closed and she was doing the meditating thing she did when she was tuning the world out.

The question of Tenzin's mental state was one Ben had thought long and hard over.

She was crazy. That had never been in question. Ben figured that anyone who'd lived as long as Tenzin and seen a fraction of what he imagined—and Ben had a vivid imagination and a good grasp of history—would be unbalanced. She had moments when he could swear she wasn't even in the room with him. Moments when she'd turn to him and a second of insanity was caught in her eyes. Cold. In that second, Ben knew she didn't know him. Didn't know anything except whatever inner rage forced her to keep living as long as she had.

Then she blinked and she was herself again.

Crazy? Yes. And funny. Sarcastic. Caring. Pragmatic. The oddest combination of child and ancient he'd ever seen or ever would see.

Ben could accept it, because it was just... Tenzin. If he

didn't want to deal with it, he wouldn't spend time with her.

He knew his anger would wane eventually, and she'd have him again. The next time she had some scheme or adventure, she'd lure him into it and he'd go, knowing it would all go to hell at some point and he'd deal.

Because it was Tenzin.

Next to him, she pulled her legs up onto the seat and wrapped her arms around them, settling her chin on her knees as she gazed at the moon. He could see the slight smile curve her lips from the corner of his eye.

"You like the rush," she whispered.

"Tenzin—"

"Someday, you'll stop lying to yourself about it. It doesn't make you a bad person, you know, to like the rush. It makes you feel alive. Reminds you that you are the one who survived."

Ben tried not to think about it. Because then he'd start questioning his own mental state.

"I want to live as peaceful a life as I can in this world," he said. "Picking fights is generally a bad idea for a mortal living with vampires."

"There's a solution to that."

"Not one that I'm interested in."

"Benjamin," she whispered. "Why do you value something that only holds you back?"

I don't want to be like you.

No, that wasn't it. Not exactly. But, he wasn't ready to talk about it. Might not ever be ready.

He took an exit and pulled over. They needed gas and he needed a promise.

He turned to her. "Tenzin."

"Benjamin." She smiled, obviously amused at the gravity in his face. But he was serious. Deadly serious.

"I want you to promise me something."

"That depends on the promise." Her eyes were calculating now.

"Promise me you'll never turn me."

Tenzin's grey eyes narrowed.

"Ben—"

"Even if I'm dying," he said, almost choking on the words. Ben lived a dangerous life and there were no guarantees. Dying young was a distinct possibility. "Even if I'm dying, Tenzin. Do not turn me. I want you to promise me."

She stared at him just long enough to reassure him she'd thought about it. "I promise I won't turn you."

That was way too easy.

Tenzin hopped out of the truck before he could say another word.

"We should get tea," she said. "Then get back on the road. It's a long way to Shanghai."

NIGHT turned into day, then night again. Over and over as they drove across country. The papers Cheng had arrange for them worked. So much that, after the fourth night Tenzin didn't even stay in the truck bed. She'd only had to use *amnis* once, and that had been when the official had been more interested in the lithe young woman traveling in a cargo truck than in checking Ben's papers.

That time, it was Tenzin holding Ben back from violence.

They still drove mostly at night, though sometimes,

Ben bullied Tenzin into a daytime drive so he could see some of the country. Five thousand miles. Almost seventy hours of driving, and that wasn't counting traffic. They crossed deserts and climbed mountains. Up and over, the highway often following the same route that caravans had traveled for hundreds or thousands of years. The vastness humbled him.

Jiuquan and Zhongwei, vast spaces and mountains of sand. Guyuan and Xi'an, the Han influence growing stronger. He made Tenzin stop in Xi'an for two days so he could take in a few of the sights, but he could have spent a week there. She buzzed past the ancient belltower at night, scaring the bats, and he jogged along the old city walls as the sun rose. Ben loved Xi'an, but he knew he'd have to come back. The weight of all the gold hidden in quickly rotting vegetables made touring the terra cotta warriors somewhat less alluring.

He'd stopped thinking in English and had switched to Mandarin somewhere in the past week. Tenzin spoke to him only in Mandarin, and his spoken language had reached the point where the officials who examined their papers didn't question Ben, they just assumed he was from Xinjiang, as his forged documents claimed.

"Do they really think I'm Chinese?" he'd asked Tenzin one night, just after they'd passed another weigh station where they'd been inspected.

"They think you're Uyghur. Most of the population here has never been to Xinjiang," she'd explained. "It's the perfect cover for you. They know your accent is different, but they assume it's because you're from so far west. You look Caucasian, but so do many of the people in Xinjiang."

"That's convenient."

She squirmed in the truck. "None of this is convenient. I could be in Shanghai in half the time if I was flying."

"Oh well," he said, slipping his phone into his pocket. "Then I'd be bored."

Tenzin gave him a dirty look, but at least she'd stopped complaining about his driving every second of every night.

"What was that beeping sound?"

"My voicemail."

"Did someone call you?"

He shrugged. "Another message from Cheng's guy. He wanted to know if the papers worked."

"If they didn't, I certainly wouldn't tell Kesan."

"You wouldn't?"

"Not without a knife to his throat."

"You might want to work on your communication techniques, Tiny."

Mountains and villages flew by, harsh terrain gradually giving over to soft green. As they drove, the air grew softer, too. Cold dry nights bled into warmer ones.

Nanyang and Xinyang, where the air became so humid, it wrapped around his throat every time he left the sanctuary of the truck.

But the green. The emerald mountains and hills of Henan province almost brought him to tears, they were so beautiful. There was nothing in his experience that equaled the sheer size and grandeur of the Chinese landscape. Vast was too small a word to capture it. And the people, the cities. Ben didn't think he'd ever been to a country more dynamic. It was ancient and new at the same time.

Somewhere past Nanyang, Tenzin said, "We're in Cheng's territory now."

"Oh?"

"Which means if we have a problem, we can't rely on my connection to Penglai to solve it."

Tenzin's sire was one of the Eight Immortal Elders who ruled Penglai Island near Beijing.

"Tell me about Cheng."

She frowned. "Our relationship—"

"Not that," he quickly interrupted her. "Just him. Is he really a threat to Penglai? I thought the Elders ruled all of China."

She shrugged. "Officially? Yes. But Cheng has been consolidating power for the last hundred years or so. He was a pirate and he now holds vast shipping interests. He's a close associate of Beatrice's grandfather, actually. But he has... what is the word?" She switched to English. "He's diversified now. The Elders consider him nothing more than a nuisance, so they leave him alone as long as he gives them the appearance of respect."

"Does he?"

"What?"

"Respect them?"

"He respects their power. But he has no interest in their traditions. I think he considers them the old China. And he is the new."

"That makes sense."

She grinned, and her fangs pressed against her lips. "Things are much more interesting in Shanghai then they are in Beijing."

"So does Cheng like you because of *you*, or because liking you pisses your sire off?"

"For me, of course." She propped her feet up on the dashboard. "I'm wonderful."

"And so humble."

"I never understood the purpose of humility. It seems too close to false modesty for me."

"And you have neither."

She gave him a guileless look. "I have very little of any kind of modesty. You know that."

Time to change the subject.

Ben stretched his arms up. "I'm so ready to be out of this truck."

"Only one more night," she said. "Then Shanghai."

She sounded excited, so why did he get the sense she wasn't looking forward to it?

TENZIN hated Shanghai. She hadn't minded it so much several hundred years ago, when it was just a port town, but it had grown so crowded. Skyscrapers towered over the city. The skyline was constantly changing. There was no quiet. No rest. It was build the new and damn the past. Part of its energy appealed to her. She couldn't deny that. But there were simply too many humans anymore. A lush menu if she needed to eat often, but as old as she was, Tenzin needed little blood to survive. The blood of her own kind was far more nourishing to her anyway.

It didn't escape her notice—or the notice of the Elders—that many of the younger immortals in China flocked to Shanghai, eager to enjoy the more lax supervision of Cheng's patronage. He was going to have to be careful eventually. She didn't want to be the one to remind him. Then again, if Tenzin remembered correctly, pragmatism was Jonathan's job.

Tenzin was loath to bring Ben among Cheng's people

when he'd already attracted Kesan's attention. The wily river vampire would have told Cheng about the human she'd brought with her. Told him Ben was more than a lackey.

Inconvenient.

But not insurmountable.

Cheng still owed her a number of favors. And their continued friendship was one of the things holding the Elders back from interfering with his business. Her father considered Cheng one of his daughter's odd friends, which was fine with Tenzin. She had many odd friends. So Cheng could only push her so far. But if he started threatening Ben...

Tenzin realized that if it came down to alienating Cheng or Benjamin, she'd alienate Cheng first.

"Hmm."

Ben heard her and asked, "What?"

"Nothing."

He muttered something under his breath, but she couldn't be bothered to listen.

Ben was an amusing human, but why would she alienate Cheng for Ben's benefit?

Well, Cheng *was* immortal. If he became angry with her, she had plenty of time to make amends.

Ben was *not* immortal. And he belonged to Giovanni, who was hers.

Giovanni, who had also extracted a silly promise from her years ago about not turning Ben if he didn't wish it.

She'd promised them both. Silly boys. Didn't they know she lied when it suited her? That was the thing about having mostly immortal friends. You had lots of time to assuage their anger should it ever crop up. Ben, for instance, could barely remain angry with her for a week.

A week was nothing. Giovanni hadn't spoken to her for five years once. It had been mildly annoying, but she forgave him.

THE next night, Ben took Tenzin's directions when they finally left the main highway and drove to an industrial area south of Shanghai. He could see the lights of the city in the distance, but Tenzin said the ship would leave from the commercial port and not the city that sat on the mouth of the Yangtze River. He was itching to see the city, but he was also eager to hand over control of the cache to someone who'd get it on a ship heading to the States.

"Turn right here," she said, looking at the directions Kesan had given her in Ürümqi. "And then left at the light."

"Are we meeting Cheng here?"

"No. We're dropping off his truck. His manager will see that it gets on the cargo ship once we do. I'll inspect it before the container is sealed. Do you still have the inventory?"

"Yep. And pictures." They'd done a proper inventory just outside of Jiuquan. He'd intended to do it sooner, but Tenzin didn't want to take any extra time when she didn't know who they might have pissed off in Xinjiang. Jiuquan was well within her sire's territory.

"Pictures?" She smiled. "How convenient. It will be much harder for him to lie to me then."

"Do you *expect* him to lie to you?"

"Of course."

"Maybe you need to reevaluate your friendships, Tiny."

"Why?"

Ben shook his head and just kept driving. Far be it from him to question the twisted morality of vampires.

After he made the left at the light, he was forced to stop. The turn had taken him into a bank of warehouses, and there was a human guard standing by a locked gate.

Tenzin popped her head out the window and barked, "It's Tenzin. Open the gate. Jonathan is expecting me."

The guard either recognized her face or her name, because the human reached back into the small booth and pressed something that made the gate swing out. Within minutes, they were driving through the warehouses.

"Where to?"

"I have no idea. Just keep driving. I think these are all Cheng's. Jonathan will find us."

He didn't look like a "Jonathan," but a wind vampire swooped down and hovered next to the truck, motioning Tenzin to follow him. He led them down a narrow alley until Ben could see a figure looming at the end of one row. Tall and lean, the vampire had the glowing pallor of a man who'd been light skinned in life and was almost translucent in immortality. He was definitely not Chinese.

"Is that Jonathan?"

She nodded.

Jonathan wore a black trench coat despite the heat, and a thin blue scarf around his neck.

"He always wears the scarf. Don't ask," Tenzin said.

"Got it."

Vampires were, almost to a fault, eccentric in some way or another. A scarf in tropical humidity was hardly the weirdest thing he'd ever seen.

Then she said, "Don't speak."

"Okay. Don't kill anyone."

She threw back her head and laughed. "I suppose we'll both have to just do our best."

Ben had to smile. And he was still smiling when he stopped the truck and climbed out. Jonathan raised a single eyebrow, the hollows of his cheeks shadowed in the glow of the headlights. He was handsome in that thin, European way a lot of vampires had. Tall and dark haired, the vampire's eyes were shockingly blue, even in the low light of the industrial complex. He glanced at Ben for only a second before he turned his eyes to Tenzin. Beyond the facade of indifference, Ben could see the wary intelligence in his eyes. This was no overconfident flunky.

"Tenzin," he said in a perfect British accent. "How lovely to see you again."

"You too." She jumped up and executed a few somersaults in the air, stretching herself after the cramped truck. Jonathan looked at Ben. Ben looked back, glanced at Tenzin flipping herself end over end in the air.

Ben shrugged. "She doesn't like vehicles."

"I imagine not. And you are?"

"Speechless until she kills someone."

"Dear Lord," Jonathan said. "You *must* be Vecchio's ward."

"I couldn't say."

Tenzin flew down and landed on his back, wrapping her arms around his neck from behind and her legs around his waist, careless as a kid asking for a piggyback ride.

"He's mine," Tenzin said. "Don't try to steal him."

Jonathan's expression didn't change a bit, but he said,

"Tenzin, I've heard an odd rumor about some immortals going missing in Kashi."

"Kashi?"

Ben said, "It's the modern name for Kashgar, T."

"Oh! I have no idea what you're talking about."

"I do believe that Cheng would agree with you. Most vehemently. You have absolutely no idea what could have happened to them. Any rumors to the contrary are the vampire version of urban legends."

Ben said, "She probably has a few of those floating around already." He glanced over his shoulder. "No pun intended."

Tenzin rested her chin on Ben's shoulder. "Odd place, Xinjiang. All sorts of people pass through there. Highly uncivilized."

Jonathan asked, "Didn't you live there for several hundred years?"

"Of course I did. I love it. But unfortunate incidents happen."

Frustratingly polite irritation. That was how Ben would classify the expression on Jonathan's face at that moment. "I distinctly remember Cheng making a request for no 'unfortunate incidents' to occur during your travels in Xinjiang."

Ben said, "She's very bad at following orders."

She pinched his lips together. "So are you. It's done, Jonathan. Get over it. Especially because I have no idea what Cheng could be talking about."

"Right." Jonathan glanced back at the truck. "What a delectable scent, my dear. I'll have our people clean it out and pack the crates in the container. The ship leaves in two days and will be in Long Beach twelve days after that. I trust you have people on the other side who can take care of things there?"

"I've already talked to Ernesto."

"Excellent." Jonathan was all business. "Then we will have everything ready for you to inspect tomorrow evening. The container will be sealed in your presence and then loaded that night. Do you have your own inventory?"

"My human does."

Jonathan nodded. "Then I'll take you to Cheng as soon as the truck is secured."

"No."

A shiver crept down Ben's spine when Jonathan turned. "No?"

"I'm tired and I stink. I want safe lodging for me and my human tonight. I'll meet Cheng tomorrow. At sunset, if he wants. But surely he won't want to greet me when I still smell like rotting vegetables."

Jonathan didn't say anything. Clearly, this was not the plan. But Ben was guessing Tenzin outranked Jonathan *and* Cheng in whatever intricate political and social construct was in play here. They could hardly refuse her request without offending her.

"Of course," Jonathan finally said. "We will make arrangements—"

"I have my own accommodations arranged," Tenzin said, still perched on Ben's back. "I simply want to know that my human can move freely within the city during the day if he wishes."

"You may depend on it," Jonathan said smoothly. "Cheng's hospitality is renowned. I hope your human enjoys Shanghai. Shall I arrange a vehicle?"

"Please."

Within minutes, Ben was driving a car that Jonathan had procured for them. He didn't speak, just took the keys and sat in the driver's seat while Tenzin got in the back. She was far more comfortable in a vehicle now. Not a bad thing.

"I'll show you where to go," Tenzin said, as she settled into the plush bench of the black Mercedes sedan. "This is much nicer than the truck."

"Most cars are nicer than that truck."

"Hmm. Curious."

"Tiny, you realize this car—"

"Will be tracked somehow. Yes, I know. We're not going very far."

"You do remember I can't fly, right?"

She laughed. "We're in Shanghai, Benjamin. There are far better ways for you to travel."

Chapter Eight

BEN WOKE TO the sound of lapping water under his window and the voices of old women in the courtyard, laughing as they hung the laundry. It was early. Way too early.

They'd arrived in the small water town late last night after dumping the car not far from a freshwater lake west of the city.

Tenzin and Ben had walked to a boatyard near the lake and "borrowed" a narrow wooden vessel reminiscent of a gondola that Tenzin piloted across the still water. Night birds called and the moon was high. As they navigated the dark canals and tributaries on the outskirts of Shanghai, Ben felt as if they were the only two beings on earth.

They approached the water town from the lake and turned down a wide canal, slipping under an arching bridge before they made their way into the village. Lights grew fainter and canals narrower. There were no cars. Few humans. It was deep in the night. No one gave them a passing glance.

They docked the boat near a bridge and climbed the stone steps. Ben heard fish jumping behind them. He said nothing, thoroughly exhausted by days of travel. He followed Tenzin as she led him down one street and across another bridge. On the other side, she stopped in front of a square set of doors and knocked softly. Blocky characters hung over the door. It was a boarding house or hotel of some kind, but when an old woman answered the door, Ben realized it was no ordinary hotel.

The old woman bowed deeply to Tenzin and stammered something in a language Ben didn't recognize. Tibetan, perhaps? Like Tenzin, her hair was worn in many braids. When she bowed, there was a slight tilt of her head to the left as she bared her neck. A subtle gesture Beatrice had explained to Ben before he left for Asia.

A tilted bow was a mark of respect and an acknowledgement of a vampire's immortal status. The human who bowed that way was acknowledging the vampire and also submitting to his or her bite, should the vampire need to drink. It was meant to be respectful and welcoming, but the tilted bow of the woman with silver-threaded braids made Ben shudder. She was old. She looked like someone's grandmother. Surely Tenzin wasn't going to bite her.

The old woman smiled up at him, and Ben realized he was being introduced. He stepped forward and held out his hand. The old woman took it and pulled him through the gate and into a courtyard lit with candles. There was a large pond in the middle with channels cutting through the cobblestones that led under the house. Ben realized the pond must connect with the network of canals that ran through the town. Gold fish darted in the shadows thrown by the candlelight.

The old woman showed Ben to a small room where a maid was already turning down the bed.

"You can stay here," Tenzin said. "Jinpa is a relative of Nima's and her house is under my sire's protection. We are completely safe, so you'll be able to rest."

He eyed the dark windows in his room. "And you?"

"There are light-safe rooms for me." She gave him a slight smile. "Clean up and get some sleep. You look exhausted. There are many shops here. Some that cater to Westerners. We'll try to find some clothes for you tomorrow."

He'd been wearing the same set of clothes, alternating with a pair of too-short sweatpants and a few t-shirts he'd bought in Xi'an, for days on end. New clothes would be more than welcome.

"I'll see you tomorrow then."

"Have Jinpa show you to my chambers before sundown. We need to talk before we seen Cheng."

"Right." He didn't want to think about that meeting. He was hoping to skip it altogether. Why on earth did he need to be there for Tenzin's meeting with her old boyfriend? He blinked as the exhaustion started to really hit.

"Sleep, Benjamin."

She didn't need to use *amnis*. As soon as he'd taken a quick shower, he slept, and he didn't wake for hours. He felt the sun come up, warm stripes cutting across his back. He heard the water lapping below the house and the old women laughing as they worked. He roused himself enough to close the blinds before he stumbled back to bed.

He slept. He dreamed. And in his dream, he flew over mountains like none he'd ever seen, soaring into a black-dipped night. He saw the moon shadows of white birch groves from the sky, swooping down to trail his fingers in the frigid stream that cut through them.

He heard her laughter behind him. Above him. At his back.

Her lips were on his. Cool. He tasted honey and tea.

Her mouth was at his neck. Her body brushed his. Her mouth... He could feel her. Feel the pointed pressure. His heart raced in anticipation.

Her mouth was at his neck—

"BENJAMIN."

He woke with a gasp, Tenzin hovering over him as he lay tangled in the sheets. The heated dream caused his face to flush as he pushed her away.

"Dammit, Tenzin." He shoved up to sitting and gathered the bedclothes around his body. He'd been so exhausted the night before, he'd tumbled into bed naked. He didn't even own a pair of pajamas anymore, because he'd left everything at the hostel in Kashgar. "Get the fuck out. I didn't invite you in my room."

She frowned. "It's almost nightfall and you still hadn't come to me."

"Yeah, I was tired." And turned on. And he really didn't want her to see the evidence. Could he have no privacy? Just a little was too much to ask?

"Did you sleep all day?"

"Yes, I did." Dammit, but she was irritating sometimes. "Apparently I'm a weak human who hasn't had a good night's rest in weeks. I can't imagine why the hell I'd want to actually sleep when I finally got into a comfortable bed."

Tenzin's face screwed up in confusion. "If you slept so much, then why are you so cranky?"

"I'm not cranky!" He took a deep breath. "Boundaries, remember? I'm... naked. And still waking up. And you were just—" he held a hand inches in front of his face "—

right there when I opened my eyes. You surprised me. I'd appreciate a little privacy. Will you leave, please?"

"We need to talk before we go."

"Yeah, I remember. Give me a few minutes."

"I'll need to bite you. And then find you some clothes, since you didn't go out today and yours are all wet. Jinpa washed them not realizing you didn't have any others."

"Yeah, that's fine. I'll hit the shops—wait. What?"

Did she just casually mention biting him like he was some kind of bowing servant?

She shook her head. "No, *I* have to go to the shops. You don't have any clothes, remember?"

"Yeah, that's not gonna happen."

"But you need clothes." She looked confused. And kind of adorable. She was going to drive him insane.

"You're not biting me, Tenzin. You can, however, buy me some clothes." He turned and tried to tuck the sheets around himself. He scanned the room. Yep, they'd taken everything. Even his underwear. Couldn't they ask? Or did they just assume Tenzin called the shots and he was a servant, so there was no need to ask his opinion about anything?

Thousands of kilometers of driving. No sleep. Stupid dreams, and then Tenzin talks about biting—

"But Cheng will think you're my human lover," she insisted. "That's what we want him to assume so he'll ignore you. One bite would be sufficient. It won't hurt."

"I don't care! You're not biting me." He didn't know why he was so angry. It probably had something to do with weeks of culture shock, uncomfortable beds, and being really really hungry.

Not just for food.

"Forget it, Tenzin."

Her mouth curled down into a frown. "But if you were my lover—"

"Are we going to have *sex* because Cheng thinks I'm your lover?"

And fuck. That train of thought was not helping the situation under the sheets.

"Of course not."

"So we're just going to lie and expect him to buy it?" Ben reached out and grabbed her hand, pulling her hard into his chest. "Even though you obviously don't smell like me?"

"What are you doing?" Her face had gone totally blank.

Ben rolled them over so that Tenzin was laying on the bed under him. Now they both looked pissed. That seemed fair.

"You're saying you need to bite me because Cheng would assume a human lover would feed you. Well, I'd smell like you too, Tenzin." He lowered his face to hers. Ben could feel her gather in a breath. He was frankly amazed she hadn't punched him yet. "And you'd smell like me. Not just my blood, but my skin. My sweat. *Everything*."

"You're being an ass."

"Am I? Did I break into your room while you were sleeping?" The sheet was still wrapped around his waist, but that was pretty much the only thing separating them. She had to feel him.

Tenzin glared. "I don't sleep. And if you broke into my room, I'd hurt you."

He lowered himself so his chest was pressing against hers. "Isn't turnabout fair play?"

"A bite isn't the same as—"

"I don't give a shit what you think or don't think it is. You're not biting me. You want to pretend we're lovers?" He propped himself up with one arm and reached for the knife under his pillow. "Here's your pretend bite."

"Benjamin!"

Her hands came up, but Tenzin didn't stop him when he pierced the skin of his neck with the tip of the blade, just where her mouth had been in his dream. Two quick flashes of pain and he could feel the blood well.

Tenzin's eyes dilated. Her mouth fell open and her fangs glistened. The piercing pain at his neck did nothing to quell his reaction. It was automatic. He grew harder. His pulse roared.

He could feel the outline of Tenzin's slim legs trapped between his own. Could feel the gathering power of her anger. Her grey eyes flicked to the wound on his neck and a drop of blood fell, staining the sheet next to her.

"There's a pretend bite for your pretend lover," he whispered. "Go ahead. Have a taste. But do not ever casually mention sinking your fangs into me again."

Tenzin bared her teeth. Then, before he could blink, her mouth was at his neck. Ben felt the light pressure of her lips. Closed his eyes when he felt her suck his skin into her mouth. Her tongue swept out, licked the wound clean, then it was gone.

She was gone.

Ben rolled over, the sheet still tangled around his waist, his back against the pillows, and his body showing no signs of settling down. Sweat dotted his forehead, not only from his anger and arousal, but also because it was late afternoon and the room was sweltering. His heart was pounding and he could barely catch his breath.

Tenzin stood at the door, her face impassive.

"I closed the wounds. Cheng would only expect scars anyway."

"Fine."

"I'll go out and get some clothes for you."

"Good."

She glared, clearly displeased that Ben wasn't cowering before her obvious anger. Well, too bad. She could learn to knock.

Ben sat up and let the sheet fall, stretching his arms across the carved wooden headboard and crossing his long legs at the ankles. He didn't look away when she glanced down. Let her look. He was sick of it. He wasn't a teenager anymore, and it was time she realized it.

"Fine," she said. "Boundaries."

"Boundaries are good."

"I'm going to buy you some clothes."

"Clothes are good, too."

It was probably childish, but he smiled a little when she slammed the door.

IT was ten in the evening when the knock came. Ben was sitting in a small room off the courtyard, reading a book someone had brought him. It was a travel manual in French, but he could read a little of it. And something was better than nothing, especially with Tenzin ignoring him.

He hadn't seen her since their confrontation in his bedroom. She'd sent one of the women of the house to find clothes for him, so he was dressed in jeans and a t-shirt. He was walking around barefoot, though. They couldn't find any house-slippers his size. He ignored the knock, but heard the women rushing through the courtyard to answer whoever might be calling.

Ben was embarrassed by his anger, but not by anything else. He shouldn't have lost his temper, but it was high time Tenzin stopped treating him like a child she could boss around. Yes, he still had a lot to learn, but he wasn't Tenzin's property or her employee. And if she continued the way she had been, she'd lose any and all respect for him.

That wouldn't be good for either of them.

Tenzin needed a few people around who weren't afraid of her. Most people were either so awed or so frightened that they treated her like a mythical being, not an actual person. He and his uncle had talked about it.

Giovanni said the death of her mate, whatever their relationship had been, had opened Tenzin up in ways he hadn't seen in hundreds of years. She'd become more human. More aware of the world around her. Less remote. More curious.

Ben didn't want her to lose that. Ever. The older the vampire, the more removed they usually were from the world around them. And however complicated their relationship might be, Tenzin was one of his best friends. He didn't want to lose her to the cold distance of immortality.

"You must be the human," a voice said from the doorway.

Ben looked up. "You must be the pirate."

Of course he would look like a pirate. Of course. The vampire he assumed must be Cheng was of medium height and medium build, but his body was lean and his face must have been very tan in life. He was ruddy looking, even as pale as he was. He had a rakish grin and spoke in perfect English. He wore a trimmed beard and his shirt was open at the throat. He even had shoulder length hair pulled back by what looked like a leather strap.

"All you're missing is the eyepatch," Ben said.

"You know, it wasn't because we were missing eyes." Cheng toed off his shoes and sat down in the low chair across from Ben. "It was a battle tactic. A way of making sure our vision could adjust quickly going from full light on deck to darkness below. I believe military special forces often use the same technique even today."

And he seemed cool, too. Asshole.

Ben held out a hand. "Benjamin Vecchio."

The pirate took it. "Cheng. Just Cheng."

"Like Cher?"

He leaned back and threw one hand up in the air in a flourish. "I prefer Madonna."

Ben couldn't stop the smile. "Is she expecting you here?"

"She knows I know of this place. So probably yes." Cheng looked around. "This is a comfortable house. Its mistress is under the direct protection of her sire. She knows I would respect that."

"Would you?"

"Yes." Cheng smiled, his fangs sneaking down. "I'm reckless. Not stupid."

"Hmm."

They sat in silence for a few moments. Ben didn't speak, but he didn't keep reading his book, either. The two men sat across from each other, drinking the tea that Jinpa had brought and sneaking measuring glances at each other.

"Jonathan told me you were her lover," Cheng said. "This surprised me, so I wanted to meet you. Obviously you are not."

"Oh?" Cheng could assume whatever he wanted. Ben wouldn't say either way until he heard from Tenzin. Where the hell was she, anyway?

"I do know you're the nephew of the two scholars from California. You're gathering your own quiet reputation in our world. I noticed. Somewhat impressive for a human."

"Is that so?" He sipped his tea. "How audacious of me."

Cheng burst into laughter. "I can see why she likes you."

"Why are you here?"

His eyes flashed. "To see my woman, of course."

"I'm here."

She spoke from behind him, but Ben forced himself not to turn. Tenzin walked around the couch and Cheng rose as she approached. His friendly gaze turned predatory as their eyes met, and Cheng whispered something only vampire ears would be able to hear.

Tenzin walked up to him and rose to her toes, kissing him full on the mouth as Cheng wrapped an arm around her waist. The kiss went on long enough that Ben forced his eyes away.

"I missed you, cricket."

Ben looked back. Cheng's hand was on Tenzin's cheek and she held the front of his shirt, clutching it in her hands.

She said, "I missed you, too."

"You wait too long to visit me."

"And you never visit me, so you cannot complain."

Cheng shrugged and smoothed a hand over Tenzin's

hair. "You know how busy I am. And I do not want to intrude."

"I will tell you if you are unwelcome."

The corner of his mouth turned up. "I know you will." His eyes flicked to Ben. "Your human is interesting."

Tenzin finally looked at him. Their eyes met over her shoulder and locked. The stormy grey was cold again. He met her gaze, chin lifted, and forced a small smile to his lips.

She turned her eyes back to Cheng. "He's not my human. Come, we'll speak on your boat."

He's not my human.

It was exactly the point he was trying to make. And somehow, it still stung.

Chapter Nine

TENZIN IGNORED THE laughter in Cheng's eyes as he guided her to the small vessel he used to reach Jinpa's home.

"What is going on there?" he asked.

"Nothing that concerns you."

They both sat, Tenzin in the bow and Cheng at the stern. He put a hand in the water and used his amnis to force the boat away from the dock. They drifted slowly out into the moonlit canal, then farther to the lake. She watched with pleasure as he stripped off the shirt he'd put on to visit the house and held out his arms.

"Come."

She floated to him and settled between his legs as Cheng slid down and arranged the pillows he'd brought to cushion their bodies from the wooden hull of the ship. He'd been a man of the sea as a human, but one who liked comfort. To this day, his quarters were lush with silk cushions and down filled blankets. He collected riches from all over the world, not simply to cache them as she did. No, Cheng enjoyed luxury.

His bare arms settled along her shoulders. "When was the last time you were touched?" He held up a hand when her mouth opened. "And don't lie about that boy. I know you haven't been with him."

She thought about Ben's brash anger in his bedroom. About the weight of his body over hers. The taste of his blood and skin. She pushed the thought away.

"The last time I saw you." She allowed her head to rest on his chest. Allowed her back to arch as his fingers stroked along her spine. "I've been busy."

"Years, cricket." He brushed the braids away from her neck and kissed her there, his fangs carefully pulled back. She'd never allowed him to bite her. "You must not go so long between visits if I'm the only one you trust this way."

"You assume, Cheng."

"We've both seen what happens when the old ones become too removed from life."

"I don't like it when you lump me in with them."

"You're better," he murmured, still touching her. He was a tactile man, and she suspected he always had been. She allowed it because a part of her knew he was right. "Before Stephen—"

"I'm better. I don't want to talk about Stephen."

"Do you ever mention his name to anyone else? Or only me?"

On the boat, like this, they were honest with each other. Their bodies and minds accepting. Cheng had always preferred to have her that way. The water at his back and the wind at hers. Perfect congress, he called it. The wind upon the waves. She couldn't count the number of times he'd taken her in the water.

"I'm tired of talking about Stephen," she said. "Touch me and don't speak, or I'll go back to the house."

He chuckled. "So bossy. I'm not the one who angered you. Don't take it out on me."

"Fine. You may speak. But not about Stephen."

"Benjamin Vecchio, then."

She scowled and called up a gust of wind, knocking him out of the boat and into the water. When he rose above the surface, he was laughing.

"Oh, I missed you, cricket." Cheng climbed back in the boat. "Tell me your stories. Who have you fought lately? Other than the three idiots in Kashgar."

"They tried to bury me and steal my gold. I only intended to kill two of them, but the other tried to bite Ben. What was I supposed to do?"

"Who did they belong to?"

"Someone named Aqpasha."

Cheng frowned. "This surprises me. Aqpasha isn't a bad sort. Just young. His people are inexperienced, but not unintelligent."

"I did him a favor then, to kill the ones who were."

"Curious."

"Why?"

"I've had some dealing with him. And you are not unknown. He's rough. Young. But he's exhibited a canny ability to give lip service to the Elders without endangering himself or his sphere of influence." He stroked a hand down his face, squeezing the water from his beard. "This disregard for you surprises me. Perhaps they were rogues."

"I don't really care that much."

"I do. A power vacuum in Xinjiang could cause a political shift. Arosh has been very quiet in the west, but I've heard rumors that make me think he is waking."

"I'd be more concerned about your own people."

His hands froze on her shoulders. "Who?"

"Kesan."

He turned her around. "Why?"

She liked that about him. Cheng didn't automatically dismiss her because she wasn't as familiar with his people. He was smart and always willing to use her as a resource if it worked to his advantage. It was one of the most attractive things about him.

"It was the way he watched Ben in Ürümqi. Ben spoke up, but Kesan had already noticed him. Had already decided to mention the human with me. How many times did he mention that I'd brought a human lover with me to China?"

"Several."

"And how many times did Jonathan?"

"None. Jonathan knows what you do is none of his business unless it affects me."

"Jonathan is loyal. His interest is in making sure his sire is well cared for and protected. Kesan is looking for weaknesses and wanted to see what kind of reaction you'd have to the idea of me bringing a lover. He hoped to provoke you to jealousy. Did he?"

The corner of his mouth curled up. "I can't tell you all my secrets, can I?"

"I don't want to talk about Kesan." She turned and pulled off her tunic, leaning her bare back against his chest. "We can speak of it later." She took Cheng's hands and crossed them over her front, breathing in his scent. The old familiar feel of his arms. The blood that still pulsed in his veins when he was aroused. She felt his heart beat once against her cheek.

Tenzin couldn't remember the last time her heart had moved.

"What are you doing in Los Angeles, Tenzin?" he murmured as he lifted her arm and laid a kiss along the sensitive skin of her wrist. "What occupies you there?"

"Let me guess. You think I should be here with you."

"Yes." He curled over her, molding Tenzin's body to

his. "With you as my consort, we would be unstoppable. Ancient and modern. No one could challenge us."

"I hate Shanghai."

"I wouldn't ask for your blood," he said, ignoring her. "We are not that. But I care for you. You know this. We could do such great things."

"I like America."

"You have to be bored out of your mind."

"I'm not. I have good friends there."

"Like Benjamin Vecchio?"

"Yes."

She could feel him smile against her back. "Then why didn't you simply call him your friend?"

"I did."

"You didn't."

Was he *trying* to irritate her?

"Kiss me," she said. "Or I'll fly back to the house."

Cheng shook with silent laughter, but he kissed her. His lips were firm on her back. Tenzin turned her face to take his mouth and she could feel the scrape of his beard on her skin.

Lovely.

Tenzin forgot about everything while she kissed him. The rough texture of his beard against her mouth grounded her. Her mind was anchored in her body. She felt every nerve ending. Every stretch of her muscle and bone, bending for him. Moving in concert with Cheng's body.

This was what she'd been missing.

Too often, her mind broke free. Too often, she felt the black night dissolve her from the inside out, as if she had lost the substance of herself and existed only in her element.

"Be with me here," Cheng whispered. "In this moment. Are you with me, cricket?"

"Yes."

She closed her eyes and let her body exist in his hands. For just a little while, she could be his.

TENZIN was soaked to the skin when she returned to the house. Her face was flushed. From what, he didn't choose to think about.

Ben took one look at her and stood. "I wanted to apologize for losing my temper."

Her eyes held nothing. He didn't know what he was waiting for. Some kind of acknowledgement. Some acceptance. Something?

Nothing.

Well, he'd tried.

"Goodnight," Ben said, turning to walk back to his room.

"Ben."

He stopped, but didn't turn. "What?"

"I accept your apology and offer one of my own. You are correct. You are not a child."

He turned. "No, I'm not."

Tenzin cocked her head. "To be fair, I have never thought of you as one, even when I probably should have."

"When was that? When I was sixteen? I was already driving, paying bills, and killing people when I was sixteen."

"I suspect you were no more of a child at sixteen than I was."

What had her life been? Ben wondered if anyone knew. Did Cheng know? Had she confided in Stephen, her dead mate? Giovanni or Beatrice? Was there anyone who understood the wells of darkness behind her eyes?

Tenzin stepped closer, and Ben's eyes scanned the darkness of the courtyard behind her.

"He's not here," she said. "He went back to the city."

"Nice visit?"

"A necessary one."

All sorts of sarcastic retorts rung in his head, but he kept his mouth shut. It was none of his business.

He looked away. "If we don't need to go anywhere tonight, I should to go sleep. I'm still catching up."

Tenzin took a step closer. From the corner of his eye he watched her. Saw her eyes fall to his neck, where the marks she'd healed were still an angry red.

"Do you want to be my friend or my lover, Benjamin?"

He blinked. "What—"

"When I introduce you to Cheng's people tomorrow," she said, as cool grey eyes met his own. "When we are traveling together. You do not want to be known as my human, which is acceptable, but leaves you in an unknown role. So, friend or lover?"

He knew she would lie to suit herself. Knew it was only a question of how he wanted to be presented in her world. It didn't mean anything. Not really. Still...

"Friend," he said in a low voice. "Always your friend."

She nodded and moved to walk by him. Ben caught her wrist, bothered that the last time he'd touched her had been in anger.

"Come here," he said, pulling her closer.

"Ben—"

"For me. Come here."

She only came up to his chest, but he leaned down and wrapped his arms around her, not caring about the damp clothes or her soaking wet hair. He just needed her to know.

"Your friend. Always."

She didn't raise her arms. Didn't return the hug. It was okay, Ben told himself. It wasn't about that. He held her for a few more moments and felt a single beat from her heart before he let go. He stepped back, brushed a thumb over her cheek, and tried to ignore the blank expression on her face.

"Goodnight, Tenzin."

WHEN he woke the next afternoon, the sun still slanted through the windows of his room. Ben took a moment to open his blinds, lean out the window, and enjoy the view.

This, he thought, was the China of postcards and kung fu movies.

Sloping tile rooftops and willows hanging over the water. Boats filled the canal below his window, pilots calling and laughing to each other as everything moved through the water. Fruits and vegetables. Bags of fish. One boat full of what looked like piles of laundry. Then there were the tourists. So many tourists. Mostly Chinese. The now-familiar sounds of Mandarin echoed through the air. Ben thought he was starting to recognize a few of the different accents; the native population of the lively water town was easy to understand.

Zhujiajiao was one of the few river towns that had lasted into the twenty-first century. Graceful stone bridges arched over the main canals that ran through the town. It still got by without cars or motorbikes, mostly because of the patronage of the many tourists who visited from Shanghai. There were a few streets he'd visited the night before that hawked the regular tourist junk, but they were clustered near the main bridge. It was easy to lose the crowds on quieter streets like the one where Jinpa's house was located.

Sadly, it was only mildly cooler on the water than anywhere else in the Yangtze delta. Which meant the old water town, like the rest of greater Shanghai, was a furnace. Sweat plastered Ben's dark hair to his forehead, so he took a quick shower and dressed in a pair of linen pants and a loose white shirt that were a little cooler than his jeans and t-shirts.

Curious what was going on in the rest of the house, he slid the door to his room open and stepped into the central courtyard.

"Good evening, Benjamin," Jinpa called from across the way. She was sitting at a table near the open kitchen door, shelling what looked like peas. "Some tea?"

"Yes, thank you." He'd give his right arm for a tall glass of iced sweet tea, but hot was how they drank it in China. He'd almost gotten used to drinking steaming beverages at all hours of the day and in all kinds of sweltering weather.

Almost.

Jinpa handed him a steaming mug with a smile. "You are looking for Tenzin?"

He hadn't been, but would Jinpa actually tell him where her rooms were?

"I had something I wanted to talk to her about. Is she awake?"

She was always awake, but he had no idea if Jinpa knew that.

"Come," the old woman said. "I show you to her room."

Frowning, he followed. If this was the kind of security Jinpa offered...

But maybe Tenzin was the only vampire who ever stayed there. Maybe she owned the house, for that matter. Ben had no idea. He'd spent more time sleeping than anything else. Had Tenzin brought other humans here? Had Giovanni visited? Jinpa was Nima's family member, a niece or cousin of some kind, and Nima had been Tenzin's human companion for over sixty years. It was possible that Jinpa kept the house for Tenzin alone.

Following a narrow passageway, the old woman led him to an arched doorway with red lanterns hanging on either side. A dark green door with brass handles stood beyond the gate. Jinpa motioned to the door, then disappeared quickly, leaving Ben at the entrance to Tenzin's room.

He stood shuffling for a few minutes. She'd be awake, for sure. Tenzin didn't sleep. But would she answer a knock? It couldn't be open.

On a whim, he pressed down on the latch.

The door opened.

Well shit. What was he supposed to do now?

"I don't sleep. And if you broke into my room, I'd hurt you."

"I guess I'll find out," he muttered.

Ben pushed the door open and stepped through, closing the daylight behind him. Immediately shrouded in darkness, he grabbed his phone from his pocket and switched on the flashlight. The room wasn't a room, but a suite. Maybe a whole other house, in fact. He stood in an entrance hall lined with intricately carved wooden screens. A formal sitting room was on the right and another room with various musical instruments was on the left, filled with low couches. A tea service was set out.

You could have heard a pin drop.

"Tenzin?" he called in a quiet voice. She'd hear him, even if he whispered.

He walked through the music room and through a doorway where a faint light shone. When he stepped through, he realized it wasn't a light, but the heavy grey of a series of alabaster doors that must have opened onto an interior courtyard. The sunlight through the doors filled the room with an indirect light tolerable for an immortal. Clever. Each door stood at least eight feet tall, the translucent stone thin enough to reveal a faint glow without allowing any damaging sunlight. At night, the doors could be pushed open to allow the evening air to cool the rooms. A massive dragon was painted in one set. A phoenix on the other. The four doors stretched across the space illuminating the room in grey shadows.

"Tenzin?"

When he turned, he realized the wall behind him was filled with bookcases.

"Hello," he muttered. "Someone's been hiding all the books."

Ben bent down and tried to read some of the titles. Most were in Chinese, but there were a few in English. He was so absorbed in searching, he didn't even hear the approach.

He did feel the cold metal at his neck, though.

"I told you I'd hurt you if you broke into my room," Tenzin said, floating down to perch on his back.

Ben stood up, Tenzin still clinging to his back, her knife pressed to his throat.

"If we're comparing the situations, I'm not in your bedroom. And you're not naked."

"How do you know?"

He reached up and tugged the sleeve he could feel at his neck.

"Are you going to take the knife away from my carotid now?"

"Your pulse isn't even elevated," Tenzin said, resting her chin on his shoulder. "That's rather extraordinary for a human."

"What can I say?" Ben said, hand darting up and grabbing her wrist, twisting it until she released the blade. "I have interesting friends."

Tenzin laughed and jumped off his back, walking to a lamp in the corner and pulling a cord to flood the room with light.

"Cool place," he said, looking around.

It was a house. Not a large one, but a beautifully decorated one. He could see the door to what he assumed was a bed chamber on the other side of the library. To the left, another door that was closed.

"Yes, I like this house," Tenzin said.

Ben nodded toward the doors. "Those are amazing."

"They are, aren't they? A little joke from my father when he heard that Cheng and I were together. He thought it was amusing."

"Those are a joke? Tell Zhang he's got my name for any and all gag gifts in the future. Those doors are beautiful."

"They are. Are you feeling better? You look more rested." She motioned to the low couches in front of the bookcases. "Did you want some tea?"

"Is it cold?"

She grinned. "I'm afraid not. That is one thing I do miss about America when I'm not there. So much wonderful ice."

He frowned, suddenly realizing why her house felt so different from the rest of the compound. "But your rooms are cool."

"Oh yes. I had air conditioning added years ago. Yours is the only bedroom that hasn't been updated yet."

"You know—" Ben sat back and stretched out his legs. "—sometimes I go days and days harboring the illusion that you're nice. Then I'm reminded you're not. You're really mean and I don't know why I put up with you."

"I thought it would be a more authentic Chinese experience without the AC. Plus, that room does have the best view of the canals."

"Small blessings." He leaned back, closed his eyes, and decided to just enjoy the cool air while he could. "What's on the agenda for tonight, Tiny?"

"I thought we'd go into Shanghai. Eat some fish. See the lights. Maybe help Cheng lure a traitor into the open before he steals my gold."

Ben paused, thought, then gave her a nod. "Sure, that sounds fun."

Chapter Ten

SHANGHAI. WAS. AMAZING.

The lights. The people. The towering skyscrapers, their tops so high, they were hidden by the fog that came off the ocean at night. Dinner boats and freighters passed between the Pudong and the Bund, crossing the divide of new and old Shanghai.

From the banks of the old town, Tenzin and Ben watched the lights of the new city flash and flicker, leaning over the railing on the riverbank.

"The best way to see the lights," she said, leaning close to him, "is from the air. When the fog is in and it's dark. No one can see you if you're flying up there."

He smiled, imagining her playing in the forest of skyscrapers that rose across the river. The crowds and traffic below oblivious to her joy.

Tenzin smiled, her fangs flashing briefly before she closed her mouth. The crowd of humans was too thick along the Bund, the older European side of the river. Tourists from all over the world came to see the grandeur of Shanghai. But even in the rush and bustle, Tenzin was forced to hide, her ever-present fangs forcing her to hide her playful smile from the world.

"What?" she asked.

He leaned over, bumping her shoulder with his own. "The world misses out, not getting to see you smile."

She rolled her eyes. "Sentimental boy. Have you liked your trip to China?"

"It wasn't exactly what I expected."

"Far more exciting, I'm sure."

He laughed, shaking his head as he said, "I don't know why I ever try to predict how things will be when I'm traveling with you. But I love China."

"You'll come back, then?"

"Oh yeah." He scanned the crowds. "Though I might make my own itinerary next time."

She turned and leaned her back against the railing, watching the mass of humanity rush by.

"Is it very different?" he asked.

"Always. This place… It is always changing. And yet, it never really does."

"History repeats itself?"

"Constantly." She blinked and looked up at him. "But I can still be surprised by the most insignificant things. I am a fortunate person."

"So am I."

"Are you? Sometimes, I imagine you wish you lived a more ordinary life."

The corner of his mouth turned up in a rueful smile. "What's ordinary?"

"True. You and I, we are good at this."

"Good at what?" Ben caught a flash of face. A familiar face. The woman was passing the small cart selling cold drinks on the corner. He'd seen her before. She'd been outside the small restaurant where they'd eaten two hours before. Coincidence? He didn't really believe in coincidence anymore. He caught Tenzin's eye and jerked his chin in the direction she'd gone.

"You see her, too?" Tenzin asked.

"Mmhmm." He didn't stare. In fact, Ben looked away,

throwing a casual arm around Tenzin's shoulders to lead her away from the railing. Three tourists quickly rushed in to take their place. "What were you saying? What are we good at?"

"This." They continued walking, staying close in the press of the crowd. "We work well together, Benjamin. Over by the pharmacy."

"I see her." He was careful to walk slowly. To anyone looking on, they were two young people out for an evening stroll. "We fight almost constantly."

"Only about unimportant things."

"She ducked into that restaurant. And I'd hardly call your lack of respect for my personal space unimportant."

"Personal space is a very Western concept, you know. And I have an idea."

"Can we talk about it after we figure out why that woman was following us?"

"If you're having trouble concentrating, I suppose so."

It started to rain, a thin drizzle of warm water falling from the sky. Umbrellas popped open on the sidewalk, almost impaling both Ben's eyes before he could duck away. The woman following them was Chinese. Young. Her hair was hidden under a plaid cap, and if he hadn't been raised to respect his own paranoia, the girl would have appeared like any of the thousands of fashionable young women walking along the Bund that night.

"There," he said, spotting the flash of her cap.

"No, there." Tenzin tugged on his arm. "She gave the hat to someone else. Watch the way she walks. The way she holds her handbag. Caps and scarves are too easily discarded. But humans have a far more difficult time changing their stride."

"Got her."

They walked more quickly, following the pretty human into one of the large pedestrian streets lined with shops. Flying lights spun above them as street vendors shouted out to the children holding their parents' hands. Tempting them with flashing laser pointers and spinning whirligigs. Ben almost lost sight of her, but she ducked down a side street and caught her heel in a crack of the pavement. She paused and threw a cautious glance over her shoulder before she dove into the alley.

She's definitely spotted them.

He felt Tenzin floating a little off the ground, and he squeezed her hand. "Not here."

She muttered something under her breath, but followed him. She probably wasn't able to see the woman, but Ben, being almost a foot taller than her, hadn't lost their tracker.

"Was this part of your plan?" he asked. "To draw some attention?" They were getting closer to the alley.

"Yes. I was expecting someone else, though."

"Kesan?"

Her head whirled around. "How—"

"Who else knew we were retrieving something in Kashgar? I was mad at the time, but really, we hadn't been in town long enough for rumors to have reached the VIC. Kesan tipped someone off. And whoever is running Kashgar would be smart enough to send more than three guys after you. So Cheng's guy tipped someone off, but he didn't want them to succeed."

No one had come out of the alley, and no one else had entered. It might be a shortcut to another street. It might be a passageway between buildings. It might be a trap.

"Is anyone looking?" she asked in a whisper as they turned the corner. It was utterly and completely black. The unnatural glow of the city lights had thrown the space between the buildings into deep shadow.

"If they are, it's too dark to see anything."

There was a fluttering at his side and Ben knew she'd taken to the air. A few minutes later, there was a scuffling sound. Then Tenzin marched out of the alley with the unconscious young woman thrown over her shoulder.

Ben sighed. "So I'm supposed to carry her back to the car like that? Do you *want* me to get arrested?"

"Don't be silly." She hovered a few feet off the ground. "Take the car. Drive to the docks. I'll meet you there."

"Okay, but—"

She was already gone.

"Tenzin!" he hissed, looking for a trace of her in the shadows. "Tenzin?"

Ben sighed and walked out of the alley, grabbing his phone and wondering if there was any way to put a GPS tracker on a vampire.

TWO hours later, Ben was sitting in the car, staring at the locked chain link fence surrounding the destination his GPS had led him to. Not surprisingly, the port of Shanghai was massive, and he had no idea where he was. The phone rang. He was hoping it was one of Cheng's people, but he saw his uncle's number pop up instead.

He picked up and phone and answered. "Hey."

"Ah. Excellent. You're not dead," Giovanni said, the slight echo telling Ben he was on speaker-phone. "Injured?"

"Nope. Kinda lost. But no major injuries so far."

"Yes, she forgets the entire world doesn't see things from a bird's-eye-view at times."

His head fell back on the headrest. "So she's always been like this?"

"As long as I've known her, yes."

"And you worked with her for how long without killing her?"

His uncle chuckled. "No one forced you to go, Benjamin."

"I know." He looked around the empty parking lot. "I guess it's more interesting than spending every night at clubs and hooking up with... actually, clubbing sounds pretty good right now." He scraped a hand along his jaw. "I miss air-conditioning. And Mexican food. I'd kill for a really cold beer."

"When will you be home?"

"As soon as we get this cargo on the ship. Which is supposed to be tonight. I'll call the airline in the morning."

"Let us know when you'll be back."

"Will do." He yawned. "What time is it there?"

"Six in the morning. I'll be going to rest soon. I was just wondering how you were doing."

Well, Gio, I've lost all my possessions, I'm pretty sure I still smell like rotten carrots, and I stabbed a vampire in the eye while he was trying to kill me. Then I practically assaulted one of your oldest friends when she interrupted me having a sex dream about her.

"It's been... great," Ben said, clearing his throat. "Now, if I can just find Cheng's docks, it'll be even better."

"Why don't I have Caspar text you or email you Jonathan's contact information? He always keeps a human secretary close by. He'd be the one to help you. So, you've met Cheng?"

"Yep. And Jonathan's number would be great." Ben did a mental fist pump. What was he thinking? He should have called Caspar to begin with.

"What did you think of Cheng?"

"He looks like a pirate. I'm considering sending him a parrot for Christmas. Or Chinese New Year. Whatever. Hey, could you get me that number?"

"Oh yes. Of course. I'll let you go and have Caspar send it right away. Stay safe, Benjamin."

"Night, Gio. Give B my love."

WHEN Ben finally pulled into the parking lot near the private docks where Cheng loaded his ships, Jonathan was waiting for him.

"Where is Tenzin?" Jonathan asked.

"No idea." He got out of the car and grabbed the messenger bag that was still hanging on. It was the only thing that had stayed with him the whole trip, and its comforting weight bumped against his hip. "She's not here?"

"No."

Thinking of the human woman she had to be carrying, Ben said, "Well, that's... not good."

"I would agree with you. Come."

The tall Englishman led him through security, past the maze of containers, and into the open, where a pier that looked more like a giant road seemed to lead straight into the sea. Beside them, the hull of a freighter rose in the night, lights lit and cranes roaring as they loaded the massive ship. An almost empty container holding ten small crates stood in the open. Cheng and another figure stood nearby, a black car parked a little distance away.

Cheng nodded as they approached. "Mr. Vecchio. How are you tonight?"

"I'm well." Ben glanced up, but Tenzin was taking her time appearing.

"I believe you know Kesan," Cheng said.

Ben held out his hand, but the vampire ignored it. "We met in Ürümqi. Nice to see you again."

Kesan only lifted his chin, his black eyes gave away nothing. If he was concerned to be there, it did not show.

"So," Ben started, shuffling a little. "Should we get started?"

Cheng asked, "Did you not want to wait for Tenzin?"

He let his eyes go to Kesan. "We ran into a little trouble in the city. I'm sure she'll be along shortly. In the meantime—" he nodded toward Jonathan "—we can get started on the inventory. I have it with me."

Jonathan said, "Excellent. Let's begin, Mr. Vecchio."

"Please, call me Ben."

"Gladly." The two men, mortal and immortal, headed toward the open container. Jonathan spoke under his breath. "Do you speak Latin, by chance?"

"I do." He switched to the ancient tongue that had become a second language since Giovanni had adopted him. "I'll assume we're avoiding Kesan's ears. What's going on?"

"Do you know where Tenzin is?"

"There was a woman following us in the city. We cornered her and Tenzin took off. That was over two hours ago."

"Not good."

"My thoughts exactly."

They ducked into the container and Ben knelt down to pick up the pry bar set by the crates. He took the printed inventory and set it out next to his phone. He and Jonathan started to unpack the wooden boxes and check the inventory to make sure both matched up.

"Are there gold bars in each crate?"

"Yes," Ben said. "We had to carry the crates. There should be about twenty or so in the bottom of each. Then porcelain packed on top. Then jewelry."

"Right." He dug through straw, still speaking in Latin. "Cheng has suspicions about Kesan. That is why he's here."

"Tenzin and I had the same suspicions."

"They must have spoken about it the other night. It's possible he was the one who sent those three after you in Kashgar. These are beautiful. Very old." Jonathan was holding one of the palm size bars in his hand. "What do you estimate?"

"About two kilos each. And I think it's more probable than possible. He was the only vampire in the region who had the connections and the knowledge of where we were going."

Jonathan shook his head. "What would be his purpose? The vampires who attacked you might not have known their opponent was so formidable, but Kesan did. He knew Tenzin would kill them."

"But maybe not before they killed me. Which would piss her off. And who would she blame if something like that happened?"

Jonathan shrugged and continued to stack small gold bricks. "The vampires who killed you?"

"With the right rumors, she might be tempted to blame a former lover. Especially if he's known to be territorial."

The Englishman gave Ben a grim smile. "If he thought that, Kesan does not understand the nature of Cheng and Tenzin's relationship."

"Does anyone?"

"Good point. My God, this jewelry is exceptional. These are museum quality."

"Silly vampire," Ben said, taking a Byzantine sapphire and gold necklace from Jonathan and marking it off on his inventory. "The best pieces are never in museums. If Tenzin wanted to sell this, it would never even see an auction."

"Cheng doesn't appreciate antiquities unless he can sell them, unfortunately."

"Poor you." Ben grinned. "We like the pretty stuff."

Jonathan sighed and handed over a leather sack of gold coins. Ben poured them into his hand and counted them. It was tedious work, but he didn't mind. The treasure had been out of their control for over twenty-four hours. More than enough time for a thief to take advantage. He wouldn't rest easy until the crates were sealed, the container was locked, and the ship was at sea.

He glanced over his shoulder. Still no Tenzin, but Cheng and Kesan stood watching them. Ben's eyes met Cheng's before he looked away. The vampire looked bored, but Ben was guessing it was a carefully built facade for Kesan's benefit.

A few minutes later, Ben heard footsteps on the roof. He looked at Jonathan, whose eyes were already on his sire. Cheng stood, hands behind his back, face lifted in a smile as he looked at whoever had landed on the container over them.

"Looks like someone finally joined us," Ben said, carefully setting down the necklace he'd been wrapping and stepping out of the container with Jonathan at his side. He swung the giant metal door closed, then locked it with a padlock he'd brought with him. He didn't know what was going to happen, but he had a feeling that inventory would have to wait.

Tenzin stood, toes hanging off the edge of the container, the woman who'd been following them glaring at her side.

"Kesan!" she called. "I have something of yours."

Without a warning, Tenzin threw the woman into the air, straight at the vampire who bared his teeth and took a step back. Cheng was the one who caught the human, tossing her to the ground as her scream cut off. Jonathan darted to his master's side, but Kesan's eyes were on Tenzin, glaring at her. Ben saw the glint of silver at his waist. The slight twisting of the vampire's torso.

Without another thought, he reached for his own blade and sent it flying into Kesan's eye.

Chapter Eleven

AT THE HUMAN'S SCREAM, dockworkers and security officers came running. A small crowd gathered in moments. Tenzin landed on the ground near him. His hand was already drawing the second blade.

"Stop," she said, putting a hand on his. "Cheng wants to make an example of him."

Ben glanced around at the crowd. Mostly humans, but with a number of vampires thrown in to spread the word. All had their eyes trained on the two vampires circling each other, one with his hands in the pockets of an eight thousand dollar suit, the other holding his eye as blood dripped down his face.

"So, Kesan, you thought you would betray my friend?"

"She has no loyalty to you," Kesan hissed.

"And you do?"

Kesan said nothing, and Ben knew the vampire had underestimated the old pirate.

"I faced a mutiny once," Cheng said, stepping close to Kesan. "Do you know who won?"

"You," the other vampire muttered.

"No, actually. My crew did. I learned a valuable lesson that day." He grabbed Kesan around the throat. "Kindness gets you nowhere. Only cruelty is remembered."

Cheng threw Kesan to the ground and calmly took off his jacket and handed it to Jonathan. The crowd around the two immortals had begun to call out, clearly ready for the fight. Ben started to step away, but Tenzin put a hand on his arm.

"Wait. We must watch. We're his guests. This is as much for us as it is for his people."

"I have no desire to watch him chop some guy's head off, Tenzin."

Her eyes gleamed. "Cheng doesn't like to use weapons."

Ben's stomach turned over when he heard the crack of a fist against a jaw. Cheng's laughter rose above the cheering crowd. He forced his eyes back to the center of the circle.

Kesan was fighting back, but he had no chance against the stronger vampire. Cheng had stripped down to bare skin, the humid air of the river clinging to his chest, making it look as if the immortal was drenched in sweat. In reality, vampires didn't sweat. But for water vampires, humid air was a boon, the element suffusing the air and giving them even more strength.

"What is Kesan's element?" Ben asked her.

"He's an earth vampire."

"I was guessing that based on the panicked way he's eyeing all this asphalt."

Earth vampires needed bare earth to draw strength, which was one of the many reasons they avoided the city. Kesan hadn't expected this ambush from his employer.

"Was the girl the one who drove the truck to Ürümqi?"

"Yes. She's his servant. He didn't think we'd turn down the offer of a driver. He planned to use her to steal my gold. She was going to seduce and kill you. Kesan thought I would blame Cheng and he could use the loss of face to grab more power for himself. How did you know she was the driver?"

"I remember thinking how weird it was that the seat was so far up when I got in the truck. Thinking back, someone a lot smaller than Kesan must have been driving and it must have been a human, because the dashboard wasn't shorted out."

"You're very observant."

"I try." He winced when he saw Kesan's head snap back so far a human would have been dead. It wasn't easy to kill a vampire. You had to sever the spinal cord completely. Snapping it would cause paralysis, same as in humans, but that would heal unless the spine was completely severed. It was one of the reasons swords and knives were still so popular.

This wasn't a knife fight, however. This was pure brutal rage directed at the vampire who had pissed Cheng off.

"He's enjoying this, isn't he?"

Tenzin shrugged. "He could be called an exhibitionist. He knows his people enjoy it. So this idea I had—"

Ben sucked in a breath. "Is he actually going to—"

"Probably."

Cheng gripped Kesan around the neck in a chokehold, the other vampire scrambling to release the iron forearm at his throat. If Cheng wasn't going to use weapons, that meant to make an example of Kesan, he'd have to...

"Ugh," Ben muttered. "Gross."

"Yes, that's one word for it."

Ben still faced the crowd, but he let his eyes leave the two fighting figures under the lights. He saw a figure squirming out of the crowd, trying to remain inconspicuous.

"Oh, look who wants to get away," he murmured.

The human who'd been following them in the city—the one Tenzin said had been hired to kill him—moved the same way, even when she was backing away and hoping no one would notice her. Ben stepped away from Tenzin, who was watching Cheng fight, and stepped into the shadows.

No one was stopping her.

Tenzin asked, "Want some help?"

"You watch Cheng. I've got her."

"Careful. She bites."

The woman might not have been a vampire, but she was no innocent. She crept to the shadows and fled, running into the night and away from the growing crowd.

Ben chased her.

As he fled deeper into the labyrinth of containers, he tuned out the sound of the shouting and grunting crowd, focusing on the single panting breaths of the human who was trying to escape. Part of him was reluctant to chase her. She was human. Who knows how she'd been dragged into this world? Maybe she was like him.

No.

"She was going to seduce and kill you. Kesan thought I would blame Cheng..."

Well, that just pissed him off.

He ran to the end of one aisle, only to turn left and slam into something that crushed his nose. The woman must have grown tired running from him. She stood at the ready, palm out, his blood wet on her palm.

He winced and spat blood from his lips.

"Ow."

"So you were the one I was supposed to kill." Her eyes were narrow and appraising. She spoke in clipped English. "It wouldn't have been that bad, I suppose."

"Am I supposed to be flattered?"

He ducked right and raised his hands. She didn't have weapons. Not that he could see. It didn't seem fair to reach for his.

The woman smirked. "Aren't you cute?"

"If you think I have any American reservations about hitting girls, you obviously don't know who my sparring partner is."

Two quick jabs to her left and he'd clocked her on the jaw. Her head snapped back, but she used the momentum to spin around and duck under his arm, jabbing a sharp fist into his left kidney.

Ben roared in pain and snapped his head back, but she was too short to make contact. He stuck out his foot and she didn't jump fast enough. He hooked an ankle around her knee, throwing her off balance. She came down hard, the air leaving her lungs as he bent down and straddled her. She spat in his face and tried to twist away, but he had the advantage. She was no match for him once his weight was on her.

The woman's eyes darted to the knife he carried on his left side. "So you're going to kill me now?"

"No." Stymied on how he'd control her, he spied a length of frayed twine, oil soaked and kicked to the side of one container. He leaned over and grabbed it. "But I can't have you running around."

She squealed when he flipped her over and pushed her face into the dust. She let loose with a string of Chinese profanities.

"I can understand all those, you know," he said with a grin. "I can even pronounce most of them now."

"Fuck you!"

"That word is universal, isn't it?"

"You bastard!"

"Yep. Right in one." He frowned and twisted her hands behind her back, securing them with the twine and mentally thanking the boring weeks in the Cochamó Valley where he'd had nothing to do but help the cowboys with the horses and cattle.

He learned a lot about knots that summer.

Ben dragged the woman up to standing and pushed her in front of him, starting back toward the sounds of the fight.

"You're going to hand me over to Cheng?" Her voice was wavering now.

"I'm guessing you get some kind of paycheck, right?"

"Yes."

"And if the vampires here are anything like the ones I grew up with—"

"I didn't have a choice!"

"Yeah, you seemed really conflicted back there when you broke my nose." Ben scrunched up his face. He could already feel it swelling. "Anyway, I'm guessing you received pretty fat paychecks and the name on those paychecks was Cheng's. So, since you're his employee, I'm turning you over to him. What happens after that is none of my business."

They reached the pier. Kesan and Cheng were still fighting. Tenzin caught his eye and gave him an amused nod where she stood by her container.

"If I could," the woman spat out, "I would stab you with my heel right now, you stupid boy. Then I'd kill your little girlfriend."

"I'm feeling so torn about handing you over to Cheng

now."

Just then, a roar rose from the crowd. There was a shout. A wet ripping sound. Then a blood-soaked Cheng lifted Kesan's mangled head from the center of the crowd.

Ben felt ill.

The blood drained from his face and his stomach twisted. The woman turned to him. For the first time, he saw fear in her eyes.

"They're monsters," she whispered. "Every one of them. No matter what face they wear. You and I both know it."

"Yes, they are," Ben said, suddenly exhausted by it all. "But you and I both chose to play with the monsters, didn't we?"

He wanted to go home. Wanted Isadora's chile verde. Wanted to watch a dumb action movie with Beatrice. Wanted to hear Giovanni lecture him about his grades.

"Besides," he said, pushing the would-be assassin forward. "The worst monsters in my life have been the human ones."

"IS your face okay?"

"Yeah." He wiped the blood from his jaw with the wet towel Jonathan had handed him. Tenzin held out an ice pack. "Thanks."

Her hand tilted his face up. "It's straight."

"Good to know that modeling career is still an option."

"There will be a bump, I think. But you were too pretty before, anyway."

"Thanks." He pushed his face into the cool of the ice pack and groaned. "Okay, I'm done. Can we go home now?"

She stroked a hand through the hair at the back of his neck. "Soon. Can you finish the inventory with Jonathan tonight? I can't access the pictures on your phone without breaking it, and the boat is supposed to leave before dawn."

"Let me find a bathroom. I'll wash up and get it done."

Tenzin nodded. "Give me the key. I'll have Jonathan load the container on the ship. We'll check it there so they can keep working. Then we can seal it and be done."

"Cool."

Ben didn't see the woman in the sterile office trailer they showed him to. He didn't ask. Maybe he'd have nightmares about handing her over, but he didn't think so. She'd have killed him is she'd had the chance.

Jonathan was waiting for him by the time he'd bandaged his lip and cleaned up. There was nothing to be done for the nose except stuff a bunch of tissue up it and wait for it to stop bleeding.

"Hey."

"Shall we?" The tall Englishman still looked as impeccable as he had at the beginning of the evening. A thin red scarf hung around his neck.

"Sure."

The climbed on board the freighter and up to the deck, quickly finding the container in the maze of others loaded on the medium sized ship that would cross the Pacific. Tenzin was waiting, but flew away after she'd handed over the key. Ben and Jonathan worked for another couple of hours, each crate opened, checked and marked. He ignored the bustling of workers around him, the whistles and cranes. He just wanted to get done.

"Well, Mr. Vecchio..."

Ben hammered the last nail in the final crate and looked up at Jonathan.

"Yeah?"

"I do believe we are finished. Does the handling of Tenzin's property meet your approval?"

Jonathan held out a stack of paperwork. Ben took it and skimmed over it, signing the bottom of the top sheet and handing it back.

"It does. Thank you, Mr. ..."

"Rothwell."

"Thank you, Mr. Rothwell. This shipment of..." He flipped through the paperwork. "...miscellaneous holiday decor has been loaded to my approval and handled to my satisfaction. I'm sure Tenzin will be pleased."

"Excellent. I'll leave you then. You and the miscellaneous decor should be in Long Beach on schedule."

Ben chuckled, until he realized what Jonathan had said.

"Wait... what?"

"Twelve to fourteen days, depending on weather. Probably twelve."

"No." Ben shook his head and ran out of the container, looking around him to see nothing but ocean with the lights of Shanghai far off in the distance, obscured by the nighttime fog. "No!"

He was alone on the broad deck of the cargo ship.

Alone. On the deck. Of a cargo ship.

Shanghai miles away.

"Tenzin!"

He looked around. He looked up. But she was nowhere to be found.

"Dammit, Tenzin, this better be a joke!"

Jonathan came to stand beside him, holding out the key to the container. "I can assume this particular part of the arrangement was not properly explained to you?"

He clenched his jaw. "That would be a safe assumption."

"Oh dear. Well, Cheng was quite reluctant to take complete responsibility for it while in transit." Jonathan clapped him on the shoulder then walked to the edge of the deck. "No worries. I understand there are very comfortable quarters for passengers. Quite... cozy."

"I'm gonna kill her."

The tall vampire turned, a smile on his face. "That's certainly not the first time I've heard that. Nor will it be the last, I imagine. Best of luck, Benjamin. I'll look forward to our next meeting."

Then the water vampire stepped backward off the deck, falling into the ocean and leaving Ben staring at the distant lights of the Chinese coast.

Epilogue

BEATRICE'S HEAD SHOT UP FROM Giovanni's shoulder. They were watching a movie on the giant television in the den and Tenzin was profoundly grateful their faces were not attached to each other as they often were.

"Ben's home!" she said.

Giovanni glared at Tenzin. "I was wondering. His classes start in two weeks."

"He'll be fine." She shrugged. "Sea travel can be unpredictable."

Tenzin was tempted to feel guilty about the storm that had thrown Cheng's freighter off course and delayed it for six days, but after all, she didn't control the weather. She heard the car door slam. Then the kitchen door slam. It was almost five in the morning, so the only people awake were the vampires.

And Ben.

Beatrice yelled, "We're watching a movie, Ben!"

She heard him on the stairs. He must have already been heading their direction.

"You!" Ben stormed into the den wearing ugly blue coveralls and a full beard. "You miserable little troll!"

Giovanni and Beatrice's words of greeting died on their lips.

"How was the trip?" she asked.

"How was the trip?" He raked a hand through hair that really needed a trim. "You mean the two and a half weeks I was trapped on a freighter? Unexpected! That might be the right word for it. Long. Cramped. Nausea-inducing, maybe?"

"I heard there was a little storm."

"You mean the typhoon off the coast of Japan? *That little storm*?"

Tenzin smiled. "Yes, that's the one I was thinking of."

"Do you have any idea how uncomfortable those beds are? I've spent the last two weeks in a room the size of a closet, sleeping with my knees bent every night, puking in a bathroom the size of a *smaller* closet—"

"Don't they call it a 'head' if it's on a boat?" She looked at Beatrice, whose mouth seemed to be sealed shut. "I thought they called it a head."

"Not a single person on board spoke English. No wifi. No books. No music. I've eaten nothing but rice and noodles for two weeks. When I could even keep anything down."

"You like noodles."

"Not anymore! And I don't like tea, either."

She cocked her head. "Or razors, apparently."

"I was supposed to take Jackie to her parents' horrible garden party last week. She begged me to go with her. I *promised*. She's never going to speak to me again. Because it's not like I could call her." He leaned down, hands braced on the arms of Tenzin's chair. "There's no mobile service in the middle of the Pacific!"

She reached up and tugged on the beard he'd grown. "This is nice. I've never seen you with a beard before. It's quite handsome."

"Know what else they didn't have on the ship? Ice packs. Which sucks when you have a broken nose and are trapped on a ship against your will."

"I suspect they had them, they just didn't want to give you any of their first aid supplies." She pushed his face from side to side. "Still, it appears the nose has healed rather well."

"I am *never* traveling with you again."

"Of course you will."

"I'm never helping you. Never assisting you. Not even an internet search. But feel free to ask, because I'd love to laugh in your face while I say 'no way in hell!'"

"Laughter will not be necessary. Is the gold safe?"

He stood and lifted the battered canvas bag that had miraculously survived their trek across China. "Mine is! The rest of it is your problem. But don't worry, I took an extra couple of bars in exchange for escorting the container. *And* the necklace. So we're square, Tiny. Which is good, because I am never going to tag along on one of your stupid trips again."

"One hundred fifty thousand seems excessive for two extra weeks of work."

"Don't care! Never again. Never *ever* again."

"You keep saying that, but you know you will."

He spun and stalked to the door.

"I'm taking a shower. And sleeping. Probably for a week. If anyone in this house loves me, they can make me a chicken burrito."

Giovanni said, "You do remember your classes start in two weeks."

"I'll be ready for classes. If I can put up with *her* shit, classes will be no problem." He spun around at the door. "Never again, Tenzin!"

"So you said." She couldn't help but smile. His anger

was too amusing.

Ben stormed out and stomped up the stairs.

Giovanni said, “Do you think Ben knows he delivered that entire rant in perfect Mandarin?”

Beatrice shook her head. “Probably not thinking about it at the moment.”

“He sounds so much better,” Tenzin said.

“You’re right. He sounds like a native.”

“Two weeks with no company but Chinese sailors will do that for you.”

Beatrice added, “I imagine he’s picked up some rather interesting vocabulary, too.”

“True.”

Tenzin turned back to the television, where several buildings were blowing up in a completely unrealistic manner.

Ben just needed a little time to calm down. He became so cranky when he didn’t get enough sleep.

He could thank her later.

THE END

Dear Readers,

A few years ago, I wrote these words at the back of *A Fall of Water*:

"Tenzin?"

"Yes?"

"I'm bored."

"Me, too."

And then I promptly frustrated many of you by writing about everyone *except* Ben and Tenzin.

You've just read the beginning of something I've been planning for a while. I hope you noticed the title of this novella, because underneath, there's a very important little phrase: *An Elemental* ***Legacy*** *Novella.*

That's right, far from having one book, Benjamin Vecchio will be the main character in his very own series, the Elemental Legacy series.

It wasn't something I'd planned when I first wrote that skinny twelve-year-old boy in *This Same Earth*, but Ben has grown into a character I love just as much (and probably more) as any other featured in the Elemental World. I've watched him grow up in my mind and in my books, and I can't wait to feature him in a brand new series. Lots of your favorite past characters will be featured, just as they were in this story, along with many new ones. The Elemental universe is a big place, and I can't wait to show you some of its other secrets.

And for those of you who might be wondering, please don't fear that this series is going to be Elemental Mysteries 2.0. I loved Giovanni and Beatrice's story, but Ben is his own character, and he has his own path to take. I think you can tell by this story that—no matter what he may claim—Ben has a big appetite for adventure. And you know your favorite wind vampire will be along to add levity, wisdom, and more than a little mayhem into any scheme Ben might plan.

I'll still be continuing to write in the Elemental World, so don't fear that any story lines have been dropped. The Elemental Legacy series is still in the planning stages, but I wanted to give you a preview of what the future holds.

I hope you enjoyed *Shadows and Gold*.

Thanks for reading,

Elizabeth

Continue reading for a free preview of

IMITATION AND ALCHEMY

The next novella in the Elemental Legacy series

Prologue

BENJAMIN VECCHIO SAT IN THE library of his home in Pasadena, studying for his art history final. To say the class was an easy A would be a gross understatement, but the habits instilled by his scholar of an uncle wouldn't allow him to rest for the night until he'd at least looked over his notes.

A small air vampire floated into the room and over the library table, blocking his notebook. She settled on his textbook and waited silently for Ben to acknowledge her.

He glanced up at Tenzin a second before he shook his head. "Nope."

She said nothing, watching Ben with storm-grey eyes that always seemed just a little out of place. Her features were unquestionably born on the steppes of Central Asia. Her full lips remained closed over the lethal, clawlike fangs in her mouth. And her expression? It revealed nothing.

"Whatever it is," he continued, "the answer is no. I can't spar tonight. I have a final tomorrow. And I don't have time to get online and research an obscure manuscript in Sanskrit or whatever it is you want. I need to sleep."

The air vampire continued to watch him silently. Ben continued to ignore her. Ignoring Tenzin when she wanted something from him was a talent he'd been honing for years.

She had a face that could have been fifteen or thirty, depending on her expression. She'd let her hair grow out to below her shoulders the past few years, so she looked younger than Ben now. If you didn't know who or what she was, she could pass herself off as an innocent schoolgirl.

Well, until she smiled and you saw the fangs.

She used her looks to her advantage, but no matter what expression Tenzin wore, Ben saw the millennia when he looked into her eyes.

She ignored his indifference and leaned over his notes. "Why are you studying this? You knew about neoclassicism before I met you."

He grimaced. Modern universities were inexplicable to Tenzin. "I need the credits if I'm going to graduate next winter. I only have one more semester, and I've ignored most of my lower-level requirements."

"Because they are stupid."

"Art history is not stupid."

She flicked the edge of his notebook. "Taking a class where you probably know more than the instructor is stupid."

"Well, they wouldn't let me take the upper-level class."

"Why not?"

"Because I hadn't taken the lower level... Listen"—he sat back in his chair—"do you have a purpose here? What do you want?"

"It doesn't matter." She shrugged. "You've already said no."

"Tenzin—"

"Why are you taking art history?" She stretched out on the table, lazing like a cat. "What does art history have to do with political science?"

"Nothing. It's just part of my— Will you get off that?" He pulled his textbook from under her hair. "I need to study—"

"No, you don't! You've known art since you were old enough to steal it. Do you want some food? I feel like cooking. What would you like? I'll cook food and you can eat it."

"What do you want, Tenzin?"

She rolled over and propped her chin on her hands; her eyes laughed at him. "You already said no."

"Just tell me."

She kicked her legs. "I want to go to Italy this summer."

His eye twitched and he looked back to his book. "No."

"You go to Italy all the time."

"I learned my lesson last summer, Tiny."

"We're not going to China. I want to go to Italy. It's practically a second home to you. You have a house in Rome."

"*Gio* has a house in Rome. If you want to borrow it, ask him."

"You speak Italian like a native. You have friends there. You could visit Fabia."

"Fabia has a boyfriend lately."

"So?"

"Just... no."

She didn't move from her position stretched on the table. Not even when he picked up his notes and stood them up, blocking her face.

"What if—"

"No!" He slammed his notebook down. "No. No. No. I'm not getting involved in one of your schemes. I'm not stealing anything. I'm not pretending to be your butler again—"

"I only told one person that, and I think Jonathan knew it was a joke."

"I do not want to lie to dangerous people. I don't want to run for my life. I don't want to hurt anyone. I don't want to get beat up or threatened or—"

"Fine!" She scowled and lay on her back, huffing at the ceiling. "What happened to you? You used to be fun."

"I grew up, Tenzin. And I realized that I can't live in my aunt and uncle's house forever. I'm twenty-two. I'm going to have to get a job one of these days. And a house. And pay bills." Ben grimaced. "I'm going to have to figure out something useful to do with my life, and I have no idea what the hell that means for someone like me."

He slammed his notes back on the table and tried to concentrate, all the while feeling her eyes on him like a brand.

After a few minutes, she crawled across the table and leaned down to his ear. Tenzin whispered, "Medieval gold coins from Sicily."

He groaned and let his head fall back. "I hate you a little right now."

❂

GIOVANNI was in the den, curled up with a book, Beatrice lying across his legs while she caught a movie.

Ben stopped in the doorway and watched them.

It was a hell of a lot to aspire to. Some days his heart ached watching them. As much as they loved him—and he knew his aunt and uncle loved him a lot—the love they had for each other was so tangible it almost hurt. He couldn't imagine having love like that. If he ever did, he'd grab on to it with everything he had.

Ben would never forget the months they spent in Rome when he was sixteen. When Giovanni had been taken, leaving Beatrice alone. It was the first time he ever remembered feeling stronger than his aunt.

Giovanni looked up with a smile. "Hello."

"Hey."

Beatrice stretched her legs and kicked a pillow off the end of the couch. "What are you doing tonight? Come sit with us."

Ben walked over and sat down. "I was just studying. Two more finals before summer break."

Beatrice smiled. "I'm so proud of you. Have I told you that lately? We're both so proud of you. I can't believe you've almost earned your degree."

He glanced at their loving smiles before he turned away in embarrassment. "Thanks."

Beatrice was thirty-eight now but looked barely older than Ben.

It was odd to realize that in a few years he would be the one who looked older than his aunt. Their relationship was already changing, becoming more friendly than parental. Just another reminder that time was passing.

Too fast, a childish voice whispered inside. *Too fast!*

"What do you think you want to do this summer?" Giovanni asked. "You should do something fun. Beatrice and I are stuck here, working on that damned library theft." He added a string of Latin curses that had Beatrice smoothing her thumb over his lips.

"Shhhh," she said. "You'll shock the boy."

"I don't think that's possible anymore," Giovanni said.

Ben had forgotten all about the library heist when he was thinking about how to sneak off to Italy without his uncle becoming suspicious.

It had been a massive scandal in the rare-book world and had become the bane of his uncle's existence since much of the "uncatalogued special collections" that had been stolen from the Girolamini Library in Naples wasn't actually part of the library but was instead the private collections of numerous Italian immortals. Some of the vampires had stored their private miscellany in the library since the sixteenth century and did not take kindly to humans stealing and selling their treasured manuscripts or personal papers.

Giovanni and Beatrice had been hired by multiple clients to track down particularly elusive items that had made their way onto the black market. The Naples library heist had been keeping them—along with their resident librarians in Perugia, Zeno and Serafina—busy on and off for almost two years.

Ben cleared his throat. "It's funny you mentioned Naples. I was actually thinking of going to Italy for part of my break."

Beatrice frowned. "In the summer? But it's so hot! You sure you don't want to go down to Chile?"

"I haven't seen my friends there since Christmas. And Fabi's seeing a guy she wanted me to meet. So—"

"The house in Rome is yours anytime you want,"

Giovanni said. "You know that. In fact..." He frowned. "If you don't mind doing some work while you're there, I think Zeno will be in Rome the middle of June working at the Vatican Library. I might have you take some notes to him."

"And that journal we tracked down in New York last month," Beatrice said. "Ben can take that to Zeno too. Collect on that commission."

"Good idea, Tesoro," he murmured, brushing her dark hair from her cheek. "Ben, let me know if you want to borrow the plane. But right now—"

"Got it." He stood when he saw Beatrice turning to her mate. "I know when I'm not wanted."

"Close the door on the way out."

Glancing over his shoulder, Ben saw Giovanni had already pulled Beatrice to straddle him. He tried not to laugh.

Like rabbits, the two of them.

"Ben—" Giovanni pulled his lips from his mate's and cleared his throat. "I'll let Emil know you'll be in Rome this summer. You know the game. Just make sure you stay out of Naples."

Ben's Tenzin-radar went off. Naples. Southern Italy. Sicily. Very southern Italy...

Medieval *Sicilian* coins, huh?

"What's up with Naples?" he asked, trying to sound casual. "Problems with the VIC?"

"The 'vampire in charge' as you say, is named Alfonso. He's Spanish. Or Hungarian. I'm not sure. And he's..." Giovanni frowned.

"He's nuts," Beatrice threw out. "Completely bonkers. And mean. He hates Emil."

"Ah." Ben nodded. "Big Livia supporter?"

Beatrice said, "No, he hated Livia too."

Giovanni was watching his mate with the focused stare that told Ben he'd forgotten anyone but Beatrice was in the room. It was the vampire hunting stare, and Ben knew if he didn't get out of the den quickly, he was going to see way more of his aunt and uncle than he wanted.

"Just..." Beatrice held Giovanni back. "Stay out of Naples. It's not a good idea right now. The rest of the country? No problem."

"Avoid Naples." He gave them a thumbs-up they probably didn't see. "Got it. Later. Don't do anything I wouldn't do. Except, you know, the biting stuff I don't want to know about."

"Good night, Benjamin."

He shut the double doors behind him and leaned back, letting out a long breath before he walked to his bedroom. "How much you want to bet...?"

THE next night, he was working with Tenzin at her warehouse in East Pasadena. She'd converted most of the old building to a training area, complete with one full wall of weapons. The only personal space was a loft in the rafters with no ground access.

Because the only person allowed up there could fly.

The windows were blacked out, which made life easier when you didn't sleep. At all. Ben didn't know how she stayed sane. Then again, the state of Tenzin's sanity was never a settled subject.

"Look at that." She leaned over his shoulder and reached her finger toward the computer screen, which began to flicker before he slapped her hand away.

"Don't touch."

They were watching a video about Kalaripayattu, an obscure Indian martial art, that someone had posted on YouTube. Tenzin *adored* YouTube.

"But look at those forms," she said. "So much similarity to modern yoga. But more..."

"Martial."

"Yes, exactly. If you could isolate pressure points..."

She started muttering in her own language, which no one but Tenzin and her sire spoke anymore, though Ben thought he was starting to pick up some words. Giovanni theorized it was a proto-Mongolian dialect of some kind, but Ben only spoke Mandarin. He hadn't delved into Central or Northern Asian languages yet.

"If you watch..." She frowned. "The balance. That is key. This is very good. We'll incorporate some of the balance exercises for you since you are top-heavy now."

"It's called muscular, and it's a product of testosterone. I refuse to apologize for that."

"Look." She slapped his arm. "The short-stick fighting. We can incorporate some of those techniques too."

"Are you saying I have a short stick?"

She frowned, still staring at the computer screen. "What are you talking about?"

Ben tried to stifle a smile. She could be so adorably clueless for a woman with thousands of years behind her. "Nothing. Ignore me."

"Oh!" She laughed. "Was that a sexual joke? That was funny. But your stick is not short, Benjamin." She patted his arm. "You have nothing to be worried about."

"Thanks. That's... comforting." He cleared his throat. "So, I told Gio I was heading to Italy for the summer. He said the house in Rome is mine as long as I help Zeno out with some stuff at the Vatican while I'm there."

"That's good." She cocked her head, her eyes still stuck on the video playing. "Can you skip ahead to the dagger fighting?"

"Yeah." He found the section that was her favorite. "So, Tiny, when you said that we'd be looking for Sicilian coins, did you mean we'll be going to Sicily?"

"Don't be ridiculous," she said, leaning closer to the screen. "We're going to Naples. That's where the gold is. Or where it was."

"Of course it is."

"Is Naples going to be a problem?"

"With you, Tenzin?" Ben leaned back and crossed his arms. "There's really no way of knowing."

Read the books that launched a fictional universe:

THE ELEMENTAL MYSTERIES

A Hidden Fire

This Same Earth

The Force of Wind

A Fall of Water

The Elemental Mysteries, where history and the paranormal collide, and where no secret stays hidden forever. Join five hundred-year-old rare book dealer, Giovanni Vecchio, and librarian, Beatrice De Novo, as they travel the world in search of the mystery that brought them together, the same mystery that could tear everything they love apart.

"Elemental Mysteries turned into one of the best paranormal series I've read this year. It's sharp, elegant, clever, evenly paced without dragging its feet and at the same time emotionally intense." —NOCTURNAL BOOK REVIEWS

"An enticing and addictive epic." —Douglas C. Meeks, WICKED SCRIBES

"A tantalyzing paranormal romance, full of mystery and intrigue. One of the best books I've read in a long time. Sign me up for book two!"—Nichole Chase, NYT bestselling author of The Dark Betrayal Trilogy

Available at all major retailers.

ELIZABETH HUNTER is a contemporary fantasy, paranormal romance, and contemporary romance writer. She is a graduate of the University of Houston Honors College and a former English teacher. She once substitute taught a kindergarten class, but decided that middle school was far less frightening. Thankfully, people now pay her to write books and eighth-graders everywhere rejoice.

She currently lives in Central California with her son, two dogs, many plants, and a sadly dwindling fish tank. She is the author of the *Elemental Mysteries* and *Elemental World* series, the *Cambio Springs* series, the *Irin Chronicles*, and other works of fiction.

ALSO BY ELIZABETH HUNTER

The Elemental Mysteries Series

A Hidden Fire
This Same Earth
The Force of Wind
A Fall of Water
All the Stars Look Down (novella)

The Elemental World Series

Building From Ashes
Waterlocked (novella)
Blood and Sand
The Bronze Blade (novella)
The Scarlet Deep
Beneath a Waning Moon (novella)
A Stone-Kissed Sea

The Elemental Legacy Series

Shadows and Gold
Imitation and Alchemy
Omens and Artifacts

<u>The Cambio Springs Series</u>

Long Ride Home (short story)
Shifting Dreams
Five Mornings (short story)
Desert Bound
Waking Hearts

<u>The Irin Chronicles</u>

The Scribe
The Singer
The Secret
The Staff and the Blade

<u>Contemporary Romance</u>

The Genius and the Muse

47000322R00103

Made in the USA
San Bernardino, CA
19 March 2017